BUt 895

W9-DGX-690

"Not that the story need be long, but it will take a long while to make it short."
— Henry David Thoreau

Inspecting the Vaults

Eric McCormack was born in a small village in Scotland. He moved to Canada in 1966 and attended the University of Manitoba. Since 1970 he has taught English at St Jerome's College, Waterloo, Ontario, specializing in Seventeenth Century and Contemporary Literature. The stories included in this book have been written over a number of years. Many have appeared in various literary magazines, but this is the first collection of McCormack's work.

INSPECTING THE VAULTS

Eric McCormack

Penguin Books

Penguin Books Canada Limited, 2801 John Street, Markham, Ontario, Canada, L3R 1B4
Penguin Books Ltd., Harmondsworth, Middlesex, England
Penguin Books, 40 West 23rd Street, New York, New York 10010 U.S.A.
Penguin Books Australia Ltd., Ringwood, Victoria, Australia
Penguin Books (N.Z.) Ltd., Private Bag, Takapuna, Auckland 9, New Zealand

First published by Penguin Books Canada Limited, 1987

Manufactured in Canada

Canadian Cataloguing in Publication Data
McCormack, Eric P.
  Inspecting the vaults

(Penguin short fiction)
ISBN 0-14-009636-1

I. Title.   II. Series

PS8575.C67I68 1987   C813'.54   C86-094644-4
PR9199.3.M236I68 1987

Acknowledgements

The following stories first appeared in the following publications: "The Fragment," "Edward and Georgina," "Captain Joe," "Inspecting the Vaults," *New Quarterly;* "The One-Legged Men," *Interstate;* "No Country for Old Men," "Knox Abroad," *Prism International;* "The Swath," "The Hobby," "A Train of Gardens," Parts I & II, *Gamut;* "Twins," *Malahat Review;* "The Fugue," *West Coast Review;* "Sad Stories in Patagonia," *Magic Realism and Canadian Literature: Essays and Stories,* University of Waterloo Press.

— To those who cared —

Contents

Introduction

I heard recently about an elderly man in some gulag. He had endured solitary confinement for many years, for a forgotten political crime. The only light that ever brightened his cold cell would occur briefly at midnight every night. The guard on duty would pull a switch to turn on the recessed ceiling bulbs in all of the cells, then he would stroll along the stone corridor to check the prisoners. The elderly man was always ready. As soon as the light came on, even though the glare stung his eyes, he would force them to focus on the page of a book he was holding, and try to read a sentence or two. The guard would peer in through the grill, slide it back shut, and move on to the next cell. The entire process would take about two minutes. Then darkness again for another twenty-four hours.

For those who enjoy reading, the idea is nightmarish. To be deprived in this way of one of the major pleasures in life seems an unendurable torment. The elderly man is a heroic lover of books, his fate pathetic. What book, we wonder, is he reading? How many years will it take him to get through, say, *Crime and Punishment* (that's the one I think he has), or *Being and Nothingness* (God forbid) at such a rate?

The story of the prisoner in the gulag is testimony to the power of the written word. In the Scottish village where I was born, I had my first experience of that same power. The people were workers without much education (a neighbour asked my mother what "definitely" meant, in a War Office telegram that said her husband was "definitely missing in action"), and they admired the ability to use words well. When I was about five or six, a letter arrived for my father from an uncle in London. After our family had read it over a hundred times — learnt it by heart almost — I got hold of it, fairly tattered by this time, and kept it with me for weeks, reading choice parts to anyone who'd listen. When that thrill wore off, I traded the letter to Phil Duffy, a schoolmate, for something I had never owned — a penknife (it had a fine bone handle, but the blades were broken). It was a fair exchange. No one in his family had ever received a private letter, and they were grateful for even a vicarious one at last.

That was my first literary transaction, a fairly mercenary one.

Till I was twenty-six, Canada was a fantasy known to me only through films, TV and books. When I arrived here, I could hardly believe the beauty of the place. Were these real trees, squirrels, cars, buses, houses? Were these people real? I couldn't keep my eyes off them, the way they moved, smiled. The men were manly, the women absurdly beautiful. Their voices were soothing to the soul and the ear of a man who'd spent a lifetime amidst the chain-saw burr and the violent glottal stops of Scottish speech. And the size of the place: on the train west from Montreal, I was convinced that one lake after another must be Lake Superior, they seemed so huge after the "great lakes" of Scotland — Loch Lomond and Loch Ness.

Eventually, in the Winnipeg winter of 1966, less pleasant realities struck. For the first time, my bare eyeballs felt the pain caused by freezing cold air. The hairs in my nose turned into wire. And that winter, my good Scottish overcoat, with its foam rubber lining, actually split in halves, right down the join at the back, when I took it off. It lay there on the floor like the broken shell of a dead sea-creature. I think now I was shedding more than just a Scottish coat that day.

I've lived and worked in Canada for more than twenty years now. I'm taken by surprise when someone comments on my accent. I can't hear it any more. But perhaps my writing still has it. Many of my stories, I think, dabble in the marginal, slightly alien areas of everyday experience — such as that of the elderly man in the gulag. The need to write about them is probably like the need to drink whisky, or to take drugs, or to do all three at the same time. And the reasons for the need are as complex. The writer may be in love, or in love with words. He may be in despair at the state of the world, or at his own state. Or he may be, in a roundabout way, just celebrating, having a great time. Perhaps it's his way of shouting his hurrahs for being, at last, by the purest of luck, in a good place. For many of us who are travellers, in mind or in body, that's what Canada is — one of the last of the good places.

Inspecting the Vaults

Inspecting the Vaults

I

The founders of this settlement have built it near the fjord, on the edge of a ravine whose sides are crumbling like stale cake. But the buildings are solid. They squat upon spacious "vaults," as they like to call them here, not "basements," and especially not "dungeons" — a most unsuitable word. The housekeepers, in particular, who live in the upper, visible parts of the buildings, stress their pride in conditions below ground. I would not deny that these vaults are "well-appointed," fitted with "most mod cons." I have inspected them all and can testify that certain comforts — a wooden frame, say, with a straw mattress; a cold water spigot, low in the cement wall; even the occasional roughly made book-case or table — are ungrudgingly supplied. Yet there are times when, no matter how generous the efforts made at muffling sound — twelve-inch-thick layers of insulation, for example, or cheerful military marches played non-stop over the PA system — the anguish of one of the vault-dwellers, as they like to call them here, penetrates all barriers, the howling insinuates itself into the ears of the passer-by. It should be physically impossible for the other vault-dwellers, underground, to hear the cry, yet invariably they all take it up. Yes, they all take up the cry, so that it mingles with the wind's constant whine down the ravine, along the great slit of the fjord, and it exposes, beyond all dispute, the fact of their unhappiness.

This, then, is the settlement, a place of many zones, built all along the ravine on land that once was forest. Each zone consists of six buildings, each with a vault, and one other house where the inspector lives. For each zone has its official inspector who lives in a seventh building that looks similar to the others but lacks a vault. The name-plate "INSPECTOR" is nailed to its front door.

The buildings of my zone (I am the inspector) rim the jagged edge of the ravine like sutures on a wound. My task is suitable for a man of retiring disposition. I inspect the vaults of the six houses once a month, then write a report which is picked up by the official courier at the end of each month, assuring the administration that the housekeepers are efficient, the vault-dwellers well looked after. The rest of the time I spend in my own house, reading, or writing my journal, for the administration discourages all outdoor activities, all movement between zones. No social gatherings of the housekeepers take place — none, at least, to which I have ever been invited.

Inspections are necessary. Experience has shown that we cannot always trust the housekeepers. They never fail to smile, to reassure me when I inquire about the vault-dwellers. They shake their heads disarmingly at my concern, they are quick with appropriate phrases: "…quite happy…," "…turn for the better…," even "…soon be on the mend…." If I stare long enough into their friendly eyes, however, I begin to feel uncomfortable.

The houses are a uniform brown in accordance with administration guidelines — last year the prescribed colour was dark blue. These houses have no windows, no eavestroughing. Gardens are forbidden. As a result, the untrained eye would have difficulty distinguishing one house from the other. The housekeepers, therefore, take pride in the *names* they have given their houses. They have named each house individually, burning the letters into wooden shingles they hang above their front doors. In this way, each house achieves some uniqueness in a landscape whose identifying features have been minimized. The great forest and the earth around the houses have been levelled. High brown canvas backdrops curtain the zones from the ravine and from each other. No effort has been made to tamper with the distant roar of the sea battering the cliffs of the fjord, for though that sound is irregular, it embraces all of the buildings without distinction.

On inspection days, I always begin my round of visitations during a period when no wailing has erupted for some time — "a quiet spell," they like to call it. On some days, if the wailing is incessant, I cancel the inspection. "Timing is all," was the final advice my predecessor, a man with a sure touch in such matters, passed on. "No inspector can survive if his visits coincide with the wailing. No matter how strong-willed he may be, the wailing will undermine him."

I knock, as always, first on the brown painted door of *Trade Winds* — a peculiar name for a house that sits within a hundred miles of the tundra.

The door swings open. A rather heavy, round-faced, middle-aged woman welcomes me. She tries to look surprised, although I am expected — mine are the only visits she will receive in the year. Always, I encounter the same ritual: a plain woman or a fresh-faced, wiry man, both honest-looking, both accustomed to looking honest. Always they beckon me into the dim interior with its dark mahogany furniture, its absence of mirrors. Always they press me to sit in the overstuffed armchair. Always they insist I share the pot of tea they have just, by coincidence, brewed. Always I refuse.

I remember how, on my first inspection of the zone, I expressed to the housekeepers of *Trade Winds* my surprise at the name of their house. I asked them how they came to choose such a name in such a place. The plain woman, or the wiry man, I cannot now remember which, laughed heartily, and assured me the name was the most natural thing in the world, absolutely the most natural thing in all the world. I have not asked about house names since.

The formalities, at this point, always begin to flounder, and I am aware of the anxiety in their smiles, their chatter. I tell them I must now see the vault-dweller. As expected, they demur feebly for a while, mumbling about his condition without much conviction: "…getting over it…," "…quiet today…," "…such a pleasant chap… ." All too clearly, their eyes show how, at this moment, they loathe me.

Yet I must insist. I unhook the heavy red-enamel storm lantern which, by regulation, must hang near the entrance to the vault — the stairs have no electric light. I place the lantern on the dark mahogany table and light it, holding the match steady, for they are alert to any weakness on my part. The man then peels back the worn carpet in the corner of the living room to reveal the trap door. He swings the door over heavily against the wall. Without hesitation, I step down into the darkness.

The light gradually spills over the stairs, and I follow it down till I stand in a pool of brightness on a flagstone floor. The leaden door of the vault in front of me glistens with damp. I put the lantern on the floor beside me and slide back the viewing-grille.

The stink immediately seeps out, offending my nose, the smell of dampness and decay. The man himself lies there, on his bunk, withdrawn as ever. His arm across his face wards off the glare from the caged bulb in the ceiling. He is blubbering softly, rhythmically. There is an indefinable, shapeless quality about him. His protecting arm looks like a fallen log in an undergrowth of wild grey hair and matted beard.

I do not speak to him. I never speak to these vault-dwellers even when they wish to speak to me. For my function is clearly defined: I am to inspect, to have visual association only with them. Nor am I at all sure I could survive any other way.

This vault-dweller, like all the others, is not identified by name even in our files. But though their names have been taken away, an inspector is required to be familiar with their case histories so that he may record any behaviour that might be of interest to the administration. I am not certain yet what kind of behaviour this might be, and so, acting on the advice of my predecessor, I report everything.

This man I observe through the grille is the last survivor of a great family from the North. Over a period of several hundred years his ancestors erected a man-made forest around their manor house. From the mid-sixteenth century, the family devoted itself to removing carefully each natural tree, each shrub surrounding the house, and to shaping instead copies of them — the details were not precise, but the general outlines were persuasive — made from a kind of papier mâché strengthened in the early days with wire, and, as time passed, with plastic and synthetic supports. They made hop hornbeams and dwarf chinquapins; they made bebb willows and panicled dogwoods; they made balms of Gilead and tacamahacs; they made shagbarks and bracted balsams; they made trees-of-heaven and madronas; they made arbor vitaes and witherods; they made Judas-trees. They copied even the root systems, and by ingenious engineering techniques, inserted them into the holes left by their natural predecessors.

The results were quite remarkable — a private facsimile forest of a thousand acres, utterly convincing at a distance. No seasons violated its constancy. In the fall, there were no deaths.

When our administration came to power, it denounced all such aberrations. A regiment of the élite Blue Guards, like beetles in their sleek blue fatigues and flame-throwing antennae, was sent in with orders to scorch the forest to ashes.

The incineration began, great clouds of black smoke and sparks erupting into the air, visible as far away as the capital. The forest was doomed.

What no one was prepared for was the animals. As the fire rolled towards the outer edges of the forest, like water tilted on a table, the forest animals in their thousands ran blundering right into our men. It was not the eyes of these animals, shining with unnatural understanding, that frightened the Blue Guards, soldiers chosen for their fearlessness; it was not their *polyphonic howling* (I use the report's exact phrase). No, observers say it was the shapes of the animals themselves — no one had ever seen such creatures before. They *resembled*, in a general way, all the animals one would expect to find in a forest — rabbits, squirrels, bears, deer — but they ran in a stiff, disjointed manner, and their shapes were not clearly defined. Their strangely wise and multicoloured eyes of different sizes were irregularly placed around the amorphous lumps that suggested heads. Mouths were gaping caverns situated anywhere on the body, rimmed with jagged bone that served as teeth. Legs were awkwardly located, some dangling uselessly from the backs or bellies of the animals. When these animals stumbled too near the flames, they would suddenly melt into pools of liquid, or explode like living shrapnel with a bang. The Blue Guards were ordered to remain calm and to kill every one of them.

This man lying here, when he saw what our soldiers were doing, came rushing towards them, screaming at them, "Murderers! Murderers!" They pushed him to one side, and he wept, begging them to spare at least some of the animals. The men ignored him, and after a few minutes he was at them again, this time slashing with a machete, so that they were obliged to defend themselves and club him to the ground.

The morning after the incineration, when that forest had become a vast cemetery of smouldering stalagmites, they transported him here. And here he lies, in his odd, shapeless way. He is one of those who, over the years, has never made any effort to speak, as though he thinks that by saying nothing he will disappear. Our administration hopes that one day he will speak, say something about the birds that lived in the forest — the birds that vanished during the fire, but are still seen from time to time throughout the country, startling our children as they hurtle clumsily overhead more like flying clumps of earth than birds.

The man never speaks, however, though he often weeps soundlessly, as now, and can be relied upon to join in the general wailing.

I close the grille and climb the steep stairs. I thank the housekeepers (their relief is patent, mine hidden), and step out into the chilly air before the stifling fumes of the doused lantern upset my stomach. The first of my visits is over.

The rituals will be repeated with minor variations at the remaining houses: the same rehearsed surprise of the good-hearted, untrustworthy housekeepers, the same damp descents into the damp vaults, the same heartfelt relief on all sides at the end of the visit. We all share one great hope: that the wailing will not begin. We cannot be sure what starts it, for whilst we, the inspector and the housekeepers, understand each other, we do not, as yet, understand the vault-dwellers. Perhaps it is the secret of the wailing the administration hopes to uncover.

Six vault-dwellers live in this zone. I know them all yet I do not know them. They will always be familiar strangers.

II

The second vault-dweller lives under the brown house called *Chez Nous*. He, according to his file, is an inventor, a natural genius without formal education. He can see right into the heart of machines, this small, bent man with the wheezing in his chest, looking up now from where he lies on his bunk towards the grille. Looking up, but not moving.

He is the inventor of a compact throwing machine that keeps throwing a ball for a dog to chase *interminably*. The dog fetches the ball, returns it to an open container on the machine, which instantly throws it away for the dog to fetch again. And so on, *interminably*. No, not *interminably*, only for a limited period of time, a modification brought about after one of his prototypes ran his wife's pet Irish wolfhound to death by exhaustion.

He is the inventor of a machine that feeds horses measured quantities of oats whilst the owners are away from home on weekends. One of his prototypes kept feeding the horses till they overate. The shocked owners, friends of his wife, returned to find the horses swollen and feverish. They tried to make the horses walk off the fermenting oats, but it was too late: the animals ballooned into elephants and burst. The inventor learnt from this disaster, made some adjustments and perfected the machine.

He is the inventor of a machine that rolls through meadows in the dawn light and collects exotic mushrooms. An earlier model, made for a friend of his wife, gathered, by accident, a lethal variety of toadstools. The consequences were too unpleasant to consider.

In the capital, he was renowned as a machine doctor, a man able to heal the indispositions of machines of any sort. Members of our own administration relied on him to repair their presentation antique watches.

His wife turned him in. She began to notice an excess of bloodstains on his white working overalls whose pockets bulged with wrenches and screwdrivers. One day she saw, horrified, a thick trickle of blood seeping under the door of the backyard shed where he developed his inventions in seclusion. Our agents answered her plea, coming to the house whilst he was away on business. They smashed open his shed door and fell over the raggedly decapitated bodies of a dozen German shepherd dogs and an assortment of alley-cats piled on the floor beside his latest invention, a device that looked like a guillotine, three feet tall.

His guillotine operated in a unique way: after the button was pressed, a set of double blades with saw teeth began to sink very slowly to the wooden chopping-block below. The teeth moved back and forth, back and forth, in a sawing motion. Our agents realized that when the blades — which were still congested with fur and flesh — came into contact with a victim's neck, they would very deliberately sever the head from the body, like a slice from a roast of beef.

Our agents never did find the two human heads: only the headless bodies of two of his wife's friends lay under the heap of animal corpses.

The inventor was arrested in the city and brought to the settlement — our administration feels his skills may yet be valuable to us. He lies on his back on the bunk, wheezing heavily, and smiles as the sliding grille rasps into its slot.

The third vault-dweller lives under the brown house called *Hill Top* (there is no hill). She is still young, astonishingly beautiful, with brown hair to the waist.

I slide back the grating and she looks up towards me from where she sits on her bunk. She is unsmiling as she rises, as she loosens the buttons of her dress, exposing her full breasts and her dark sex to me. She whispers words I cannot quite make out, as though she is speaking to me from under several inches of water, and fixes me with her eyes, knowing I am watching her, though she cannot see me in the darkness outside the door.

The administration ordered her to this place after one of our most respected magistrates visited, on his annual circuit, the country village where she lived. The villagers dragged her before him — according to our files — accusing her of being a mouth-sorceress, a manipulator of spells. Two village policemen held her at a safe distance by ropes, avoiding looking directly into her eyes, avoiding contact with her body for fear that their clothing would burst into flames.

The magistrate began to question her but she screamed and cursed so much she started to vomit. According to our files she vomited up: four Moray eels, each one a foot-and-a-half long; seven hanks of wool, all the colours of the rainbow, braided together like intertwined snakes; a bone-handled carving knife; a loaded .44 automatic pistol; a dozen compacted balls of cat and dog hair, mainly ginger and black; three engraved granite rocks, each six inches in diameter (she heaved them up, they say, like a snake regurgitating eggs); an unknown quantity of dung of such animals as cows, horses, and rabbits; countless pints of blood, not her own type, according to our pathologists; a book written in a language experts have not yet been able to identify; and a parchment that contained a detailed description of this very encounter with the elderly magistrate — had he chosen to pick it up and read it as soon as she vomited it up, tragedy might have been averted. He chose not to, which the parchment had foretold.

This fit of vomiting lasted for four hours. The old magistrate himself, shocked, begged her to stop, but did not know how to help her. The spectators were too terrified to touch her.

Eventually, she could vomit no more, and knelt moaning hollowly, like an animal that has given birth to a steaming litter, her eyes empty, her face lined with exhaustion.

There is no confusion over what happened next. Eyewitnesses record that, after a while, she raised her head and said in a soft voice to the elderly magistrate, "You have sucked me dry." Then she picked up the pistol from the glistening heap in front of her, and fired the full barrel point-blank at the man's stomach before anyone had the power to stop her. And she fell into a coma. All of this happened exactly as the parchment predicted.

She has lived under *Hill Top* for seven years, and the administration has made it clear she will never go free. Now she is sitting quite still on the bunk. Now she shakes her long brown hair back over her shoulder and catches it in her hand, and looks up towards me. Her eyes are smiling. She is usually the one who starts the howling. Her voice seems able to penetrate any barrier. Always when I visit her, I hold my breath, hoping she will not begin. All that I have ever heard from her during the inspections are her seductive whispers. If I ever understood the words, would I have the power to walk away?

The fourth vault-dweller lives under the brown house called *Home Sweet Home*. Through the grille, I see him as usual, this bald-headed, benevolent-looking man in wire glasses, studying, as always, one of his frayed charts, spread out on the table under the dim bulb, his big, farmer's hands fingering lightly the fragile parallel rulers as though they were the first leaves of some spring plant.

For twenty-eight years, according to his file, in a clearing in a pine forest known for its strange sighing and groaning sounds, not far from his fieldstone house, this farmer, this kind father and husband, devoted all his spare hours to a secret task. Using only children's construction sets consisting of small pieces of plastic less than one inch in size, he built a replica, exact in all its measurements (150ft L.O.A., 40ft beam), of the *Santa Cruz*, the galleon of an admiral of the fleet in the Spanish Armada. He fitted together, without any kind of glue, according to our records, sixty billion pieces. The masts and the booms were built in this way, only the ropes and the rigging, the Manilla sheets and the chains were made from any other material.

Our soldiers discovered the galleon by accident in the dark wood during the early days of our administration when all woods, even this one fifty miles from any body of water, were being searched for precisely such objects. They spread out and hid themselves in the undergrowth in the hope of capturing the unknown shipwright.

Just before dusk, they heard someone stumbling along the path (he was a clumsy walker) without any attempt to be silent. He hummed to himself as he climbed aboard the galleon by its dangling rope-ladder. He mounted the quarter deck and entered the Admiral's state-room at the stern. Our men slinked aboard after him. They could not help marvelling at the strength and the precision of the structure. The rigging creaked soothingly in the night breeze and the smell of salt air hung about the ship as though it had just put into port after a long voyage.

They thought they heard voices from the direction of the state-room, laughing and debating good-humouredly in what sounded like Spanish. They crept up to the door, and with their guns at the ready, burst into the cabin. They found the farmer seated at a wide chart-table, poring over ancient charts, plotting out courses with parallel rulers and hand compass. He looked up at them without any show of surprise. He was completely alone.

They carefully searched the rest of the ship but found no one, not in the cramped crew's quarters before the mast, nor in the cargo hold, even though provisions of dried beef and biscuits enough to last fifty men for six months were stored there. They did disturb several large ships' rats, which scuttled overboard and disappeared into the forest. The farmer was placed under close arrest.

Our administration was uncertain about this man, feeling that perhaps he was not irretrievably lost. They did something rare, they gave him a second chance, appointing him under-watchman at the northern, sunless gate of the capital. He would be both watcher and watched.

Unfortunately, he began acting in a disturbing manner almost immediately. Each morning, as the sun laid a withered arm on the eastern horizon, he would climb the watch turret of the great wall that surrounds the city, a wall built in some forgotten fashion without mortar or machinery — we are gradually replacing it — by our forgotten ancestors. Once up there, he would screech, at the top of his lungs, "Light! Light!". The other guards would seize him and drag him away, watched fearfully by all the people who lived near the gate.

After a while, there was no option but to bring him here. The housekeepers have claimed from time to time that they hear other voices in his cell speaking to him in strange languages, but that when they open the grille, he is, of course, alone. Our administration has warned the housekeepers that there can be no other voices.

I myself will not admit to having heard anything. I know this: on some occasions at the end of a visitation, I have watched him working anxiously over his charts at some projected odyssey he alone knows about. Sometimes, after I have slid the grille shut and started up the stairs, I hear a babble of what seem to be voices coming from his vault. I never go back to check, I avoid the knowing looks of the housekeepers at the top of the stairs, and I move on to my next visit without delay.

The fifth vault-dweller lives under the brown house called *The Nest*. Through the grille I see him dangling by the finger tips of his right hand from a tiny crack in the brickwork near the angle of the wall and ceiling of the vault, whilst with his left hand he hammers a piton into the concrete. He has climbed over every inch of the vault, marking the route over particularly dangerous pitches, fixing ropes to impossible overhangs. The vault looks like the home of a giant spider.

He pays no attention to me.

He is thin like an ascetic bird, he is an albino with a red beak. His hair is long, straight and fair. His mother, according to our file, was a West African princess, his father a Scottish ship's engineer who brought her back with him to the North-western Islands. Too alien to survive on the bleak islands, she died of pneumonia after giving birth to a boy. The father died in a storm on his next voyage, and a maiden aunt was left with the responsibility of the child.

A useless task. After a few years, the pimpled and surly boy wanted only to be alone, to clamber over the sea cliffs pounded by that northern ocean, clinging to treacherous rock-faces with the limpets and the cold barnacles.

In time, he made his name as a climber. By the age of twenty-one, he had climbed all the fearsome rock faces of the world. There are photographs of him in our files, standing high against killing blue skies.

He became a philosopher of mountains. He began to talk of "climbing beyond the peak." He came to feel that no earthly mountain could challenge him. Yet he still had ambitions. "I must make my own mountain," he told his small circle of mountain-climbing friends. He found a collaborator, an engineer who loved ingenious projects, and together they planned to build, on an island by the northern ocean, a man-made mountain that would dwarf any natural mountain. They were beginning to move in the first shiploads of granite when the plan fell into the hands of our administration. They sensed the danger and immediately trans-ported the climber here.

Yet though he has scaled heights inaccessible to all other men, he shows no dismay at being locked in this vault. He never stops climbing. Even when he sleeps, he lies face down, his arms and legs moving incessantly, like a man groping for holds on some steep rock face. When I slide back the grille, I never know where to look for him. Yes, I see him now, hanging upside down in the corner, calculating all possible angles before he makes his next move. I am happy to leave him dangling there.

The sixth vault-dweller lives under the brown house called *Cozy Corner*. She is the dignified one, the little mayoress, sitting upright on her bunk as though ready to preside over a council meeting, her mayor's chain still around her neck, her mayor's robes a little shabby after so many years. The sound of the grille opening elicits a trained smile in my direction, but the eyes are lifeless. For many years, she was mayoress of a small town in the western wilderness. She it was who introduced monthly festivals in which she encouraged all her townspeople to exchange their clothing with their neighbours and adopt each other's lives for twenty-four hours (black face-masks, she suggested, would give the necessary anonymity).

The festivals flourished, according to our files. For one day a month, the lives of her people were transformed. The newly created day-long marriages were filled with love and excitement. Men who had been lifelong enemies often became firm friends for a day, not recognizing each other. Parents for a day, children for a day, found fresh delight in each other. The townspeople even adopted the occupations of their neighbours for a day: no job that lasted only one day seemed to them intolerable.

After a year of this, the mayoress and her council, delighted by the results, decreed that the practice should become permanent: the townspeople need never return to their original selves, but might forever disguise themselves as someone else, changing roles whenever they became bored.

Time passed. The townspeople began to forget who they once had been, often inadvertently returning to their original roles. In the end, all problems seemed minor, even when the bread from the baker's would occasionally be burnt to a cinder, or the plumber would be unable to fix a leak. The doctor's surgery was always deserted.

When our administration came to power, it moved rapidly to remedy the situation. The mayoress was arrested by a squadron of our soldiers, and an interim military tribunal ordered the townspeople to resume their former selves — so far as they could be established (our files hint that a significant number of sex changes had occurred).

The little mayoress was sent here, and so she sits, looking sad, though as dignified as ever. She sits here, without question, but is she the mayoress? Because of the confusion brought about by the festival, our administration can never be sure we have arrested the right person. Our policy is, therefore, to replace her periodically with another of the townspeople, just in case. In this way we are certain we will eventually have her.

III

Six vault-dwellers live in this zone, twelve housekeepers, and one inspector. It is not always easy for a man like myself to understand how our administration decides who should be the vault-dwellers, who the inspectors.

When I first came to the capital, with its strange walls and its watch-towers, I registered with the police, as was required. I gave them the name of the place I had lived all my life, a remote fishing village by the northern sea. They looked at me suspiciously as they copied down the information from my creased papers.

Late that night, two of their black-coated agents quietly forced the room door of the seedy hotel I had booked into, and placed me, quite discreetly, under arrest. On the way back to the city jail in their limousine, with its black windows, they accused me of falsifying my papers, and said that there was no such place as the village named there. I laughed: although the village might be too small to appear on their maps, it had existed for centuries, and had a population of three hundred people of whom every single one knew me.

They did not argue. They locked me up for the night in the city jail, in a small, brick-walled private cell — quite unlike these vaults. I lay there soothed by the chirruping of the cicadas. In the middle of the night their singing suddenly stopped, and I was afraid.

Next morning the guards brought me, worn out with anxiety, to the hearing room where the jail commandant, a spruce, fat man, a retired officer of the Blue Guard, presided. His face showed no sympathy for me. I was made to stand to attention behind a worn wooden railing whilst he addressed me briefly:

"We have checked your story with all of our agencies in the northern area. They have assured us there is no such village as you claim. Your name does not occur in any of our files. You will remain in custody and will appear in court again within a few days." He rose abruptly and left the room.

I was returned to my cell where a lawyer appointed to help me was waiting, a small man with a brown mole on his left cheek and a tired voice. I repeated everything I had already said about my village, remembering clearly how it had looked on the morning I left, somehow aware, even then, that it would be my last look. I told him about the little granite buildings running down either side of the cobbled street with its post office, its commercial hotel, its general store, its steepled church, towards the harbour gleaming in the sun at low tide, the pilings erect and dry as matchsticks, the scissor-tailed birds crashing into the calm water, the work-boats (one of them skippered by my own father) nosing towards their tasks like anxious dogs swimming out of their depth, the debris of old ships exposed on the oily sand like fossils from some distant era.

I gave him names, unhesitating, the names of a hundred villagers to testify on my behalf. The lawyer, the mole on his left cheek twitching as though independent of him, seemed persuaded and said he would try to do something.

Two days later, they awoke me early, ordered me to wash and shave myself, and brought me before the commandant again. He was more spruce, more grim than ever. Administration agents had, he said, at the insistence of my lawyer (I could see him standing in the corner of the hearing room avoiding my eyes, I could see his mole pulsing rapidly), gone to the area where I had indicated my village was located. They had not found any village, but they had found, there by the edge of the ocean, the ruins of what might not long ago have been a village — the outline of a street, charred pieces of wood, fragments of brick and mortar.

More alarmingly, they had found in a nearby meadow a massive mound of freshly bulldozed earth which they feared might cover something unthinkable.

The commandant now spoke, in a controlled voice, about the house, the only intact house the agents had found, down among the jack-pines by the shore.

The house was empty, the agents had reported; but in the backyard, with its trim privet hedge and its blossoming flowers, they again found the signs of a burial on the otherwise smooth lawn. Carefully, with the long-handled shovel lying nearby, they dug till they struck what was buried. At first it seemed like a large brown leather bag, but as they uncovered more of it and tried to pull it out of the hole, they saw to their horror that it was in fact the tanned hide, completely empty of bones and organs, of a young woman. It was completely intact, in texture like the deflated rubber inner tube of a car. The insides had been removed without any sign of a scar.

As they wiped some of the mud from the area of the face, they saw that it was covered with tiny tatoo marks. One of the agents cleaned the mud from other parts of the body and they realized it was completely tattooed from head to toe with columns of words, so that it looked like the remnants of an old newspaper left in a damp cellar.

The agents rolled up the body and carried it with them in a suit-case to the capital where experts could examine it.

The commandant's distaste for me shone plainly in his eyes:

"Until our inquiries have been completed, therefore, you will be held here in the capital indefinitely. Dismissed."

A year ago, on a sparkling summer day, I was brought to this settle-ment in a military jeep escorted by a motor-cycle platoon of armed Blue Guards. When I arrived here, I was informed I had been appointed inspector of this zone, and that I was to take up my duties immediately. I was installed in the inspector's house, handed the final report of my predecessor, and the files of the vault-dwellers.

These are dark times. I do not sleep well. I think constantly about that buried girl, I wonder why the administration has told me nothing more about its findings. I try to keep up appearances, for fear of being reported by the housekeepers because of some imagined grievance. I avoid (an easy matter here) any form of intimacy. At all costs, I suppress the temptation to join in the wailing. Do you hear it? Listen carefully. There it is now — difficult for the untrained ear to pick out at first. Yes, that's it, that high-pitched lament rising above the distant base of the sea's percussion, drifting steadily down the fjord, converging, at last, with the endless moaning of the northern winds.

The Fragment

The Fragment

Of all the odd things, it was a phrase from Robert Burton's *Anatomy of Melancholy* that caused my return to Scotland in the summer of 1972. A reluctant return. I prefer more exotic places and sunnier climes. After all, I put in the first twenty-four years of my life in the vicinity of Glasgow's murk — paid my dues. Some Presbyterian deity must have been tickled pink to see me slink back to that rejected birthplace to resolve a problem that stemmed from my research in a godless, new-fangled New World.

Burton's encyclopedic seventeenth-century treatise has been the focal point of my studies for some years. In particular, I have been attempting to disentangle the section of the *Anatomy* dealing with "Religious Melancholy" — an amalgam of esoteric information on the disorders that afflict the soul in crisis. Burton drew his insights on the subject from all quarters, thereby showing, for an Anglican divine, an astonishing boldness: cabbalistic and necromantic sources abound, most of which modern scholarship has traced.[1] However, a few references remain tantalizingly obscure. One of

[1] Cf. *Bibliographia Burtoniana*, ed. James Brown, Edinburgh, 1968.

these was the bait, if I may call it so, that lured me, a rather unwilling prey, to Glasgow.

In Partition Two, Section Four, Member One, Subsection Four of
the first edition of the *Anatomy*[2] (this is Burton's own idiosyncratic
way of dividing his book), the author asks rhetorically:

> Could any folly exceed that of those Caledonian Eremites
> who must ever remayne, as *Jacobus Scotus* has it, *casti, muti, et
> caeci*; chaste, silent, blind?

The passage is typical of Burton: the macaronic mingling of Latin
and English; the arbitrary spelling and capitalization; and the
rather vague attribution. Yet one might feel he supplies information enough to allow the assiduous scholar to track down the
source.

Unfortunately, *Jacobus Scotus*, James the Scot, had baffled the
researches of generations of scholars. Such well-known Scottish
literary Jameses as King James, and James of Kelso had been
scrutinized in vain for allusions to the Scottish hermits Burton
mentions.[3] The many ecclesiastical histories[4] of a devoutly
religious age reveal nothing of the existence of a sect which
adhered in any outstanding way to the principles *Jacobus Scotus*
notes. I even began to suspect, at times, that Burton had invented
the quotation and the source — as he had done on other occasions
in the *Anatomy*.

Still, I felt I ought to make one last, prolonged effort to trace the
reference, and so it was that for several weeks in that notably bleak
Scottish summer I sat in the reading room of the draughty archives
of Glasgow Cathedral. The Cathedral is an impressive, Calvinistic
pile, the spiritual equivalent of the great Victorian business houses
that stand nearby. Together, they carry the twin banners of
the Elect.

---

[2] Burton scholars will be aware that I quote from the original 1621 edition to
avoid the many errors in the so-called definitive edition of A.R. Shilleto, 1893.

[3] R. Macduff, "Burton's 'Caledonian Eremites': Possible Sources," *Cult. Celt.*
IV, 1947.

[4] *Compendium Historiarum Ecclesiae Caledoniae: 1200-1700*, Edinburgh, 1902.

For several weeks, I made no progress in my research, merely eliminating false trails. Then, one memorable afternoon, as I was leafing quite inattentively through a motley heap of uncatalogued sixteenth-century manuscripts, I came across an untitled fragment which I was about to shuffle aside when a phrase near the bottom of the page thrust itself at me: *casti, muti, et caeci* — and I knew the search was over. I read the creased manuscript with elation. It was a remarkable document. I present the entire fragment here, roughly translated from its stark Latin:

…They took us in a sailboat across the Mull on a Tuesday, seven of us, all sworn to serve the Brethren. There was no sun that day, and the strong wind drove us to the island in three hours. Some wept to think they might never return to their families. A hut stood by the jetty where the steward met us and conducted us up to the monastery by a cobble-stone path. There was little vegetation. The building was made of granite, square and strong, hewn, I think, out of the island's own rocks. The only sound was of the sea and the wind.

The steward led us to our living-quarters and assigned our tasks. I was to fill the place of a personal servant who had died, to lead my master from his cell to the chapel, the refectory, and the lavatories. My master's name was Thomas, and he was a young man, scarcely older than I. Yet the empty eye sockets made him seem pitiful to me. In the refectory I found my task repulsive, as I helped him to eat, for the stump of his tongue had been clumsily cauterized, and he choked over his food. It was a common difficulty amongst them. My master had received his castration, as had they all, before taking his final vows. For these Brethren had vowed to be *celibate, silent, and blind*. I thanked God that I was not one of those appointed to aid the barber-surgeon.

I stayed on that island for only four months before bribing the boatman to transport me to the mainland. I decided this on a day I found my master on the floor of his cell, convulsed like one weeping. He heard me enter, and with a piece of rock, scratched on the tiles in a blind man's scrawl, "KILL ME." All the while, he clutched my robe and uttered piteous grunts. I could not console him. And so I made plans to leave at the first opportunity, for it was more than I could bear. Nothing will ever make me return. May God's mercy preserve me.

James

An astounding document. How Burton came to read it remains a mystery; perhaps it was more widely circulated in his day than we can now ascertain. Be that as it may, we at last know the implications of the reference.

Clearly, in that age of widespread religious fanaticism and radical ecclesiastical reform, a group emerged which felt that words alone were facile and inadequate testimony to faith. The flesh itself must bear witness. The Brethren willingly severed their manhood to ensure purity, they cut out their tongues to make easier the silent meditation of the spirit, they plucked out their very eyes that they might no longer offend. They tried to make themselves the perfect embodiments of spiritual self-sufficiency, worlds to themselves. Yet though these blind, mute eunuchs isolated themselves from the temptations of the flesh on that rocky island, the body continued to exist, more painfully, more insistently than before. They now needed servants to help the stubborn organism perform its basic functions.

James (without doubt Burton's *Jacobus Scotus*) says little, implies much. His master was a young man (so were most of the Brethren, I imagine), one who had abandoned half measures, the circumspect compromises of an ancient church, preferring the act to the word. He and his brothers, the truly strong, would make commitments from which there would be no retreat.

But then, the doubts, the doubts. Burton the ironist, reveller in the vagaries of human behaviour, must have relished the paradox: the more a man, in his search for God, strips himself of his humanity, the more pathetically human he renders himself.

Well, I won't labour the point any more. Another piece of minor scholarly detective work, you will say. Yet the image of those Brethren will stay with me always. I am a man of books, but no book has affected me more deeply than the scrap of paper that fell into my hands that day through four centuries of darkness.

Sad Stories
in Patagonia

Sad Stories
in Patagonia

The stony Patagonian wilderness south of the Rio Negro has
always been renowned as a dinosaur graveyard. But nowadays
several reported sightings of a *live* Mylodon (ancestor of the
South American sloth) have led to a number of expeditions
from various countries bent upon capturing this last survivor
of the Age of Dinosaurs.

P. Hudwin, *Monsters of Patagonia*, Edinburgh, 1903

When the members of the expedition squatted round the camp-
fire on that first summer night ashore in Patagonia, the hiss of the
fine drizzle on the logs reminded us, sitting on the wet grass, of
damp summer nights in our own country, and the telling of sad
stories began. The leader of the expedition, the distant gloom of
the Andes behind him, spoke first. He was commander of our
great endeavour to find the last mylodon alive, this cautious man,
his balding skull pimpled with rain, this admirer of whisky, a man
who wept, if anything, too easily.

"I am no authority myself on sadness" (we did not disagree,
though his misfortunes were legendary — the aristocratic wife
whose affairs scandalized society; the pistol-cleaning "accident"
which perforated his left ear; the addiction to cards that led to the
dissipation of an inheritance one warm night in Monte Carlo),

"but I do remember seeing something pitiful when I was heading an expedition to the Mparna range in Lower Borneo.

"While we were provisioning to ascend the Central Massif, we were living in a village in the foothills. In the centre of the village a large bamboo cage stood, curtained with coconut matting. The villagers told us that a young boy, or what was *once* a young boy, was in that cage. We could all hear frightening snorts and hisses coming from it all day and all night.

"The boy was being trained as Guardian of the shrine of Rimso, the spider-god of the region. They always keep a few apprentices in training in case the official Guardian should die suddenly.

"The witch-doctors acquire these apprentices by raiding villages out in the bush where male infants have been newly born. The witch-doctors in their devil-masks descend on a village in the dawn mists. It must be an eerie sight. The wailing of the mothers is a waste of time. No one dares to defy the witch-doctors. If a baby looks strong, fit to withstand the training, they tear him away from his mother and bring him to a cage like the one we saw in that village.

"All of his bodily training takes place here for seven years. The training is aimed at completely reversing many of the child's natural physical instincts.

"They know a way of restructuring the body. It is the same method they use to train the branches of the banyan tree. In the first months of the child's captivity, they twist his upper body a little at the waist, so that the shoulders are turned slightly out of align-ment with the hips and feet. Then they clamp it in position with vines and an ironwood frame, until, after a few months, the child becomes used to that posture. Then they twist him a little further, using the same clamping method for another few months, and then a little further, and so on. They do this again and again until the torso is turned one-hundred-and-eighty degrees around, and the boy's face is directly over his buttocks. So, when he bows his head, he is looking directly down at his own heels, his right arm dangles beside his left hip, and his left arm by his right hip. His spinal column is permanently coiled, like a spring, or like a plastic doll twisted out of shape by an angry child. The process takes about five years in a normal boy.

"The villagers often hear howls of anguish from the apprentice

Guardian in the middle of the night. This is caused by the operations the witch-doctors perform upon him at each full moon to give him the walk of a spider, in the image of the god. They have a method of grafting four thick membranes of human flesh (no one dares ask where they find the material) onto his arms and legs. The membranes form a webbing at the angles of his knees and armpits, so that he cannot ever straighten out his limbs. He is forced to crouch, on all fours, like a monstrous spider, with his genitalia exposed to the skies, his chest and haunted face to the ground.

"I saw this apprentice only once, on the morning he left the cage. It was, as usual, misty in the jungle dawn. All of the villagers and the expedition-members were watching from the safety of the compounds, for we knew that by now the apprentice's teeth had been replaced with bamboo fangs full of spider venom.

"Through my binoculars, I saw four witch-doctors in spider-masks come up to the cage armed with long goads. They unfastened the gate and poked through the bars at whatever was in there, driving it towards the opening. Something tumbled out. A huge form, entirely covered in matted hair, lay there quivering for a moment, then shook itself and scuttled quickly into the fringes of the bush, grunting inhumanly, the four witch-doctors jogging behind it, jabbing it with their goads. I never wanted to see such a creature again, and I was glad that our expedition would soon be setting out into the mountains.

"In this way the witch-doctors train the body of an apprentice Guardian in public, to frighten the people. How they train the boy's mind I do not know. That part of the training takes another three years: no outsider may witness it and live.

"But these apprentices do not disappear from public view completely. After the final three years of training, they are often seen again. Some of the men on the Mparna expedition swear that while we were setting up camp one night in the rain forest under the mountain, a monster unlike anything they had ever come across shuffled out of the undergrowth towards them, grunting brutally, cowing the hunting dogs, silencing all the jungle creatures. They could see insane red eyes under a wilderness of hair. For some reason, it suddenly stopped and slithered back into the bush. If what they saw really was an apprentice, they were lucky, for, according to the villagers, its appetite for inflicting pain, either on itself or on others who stumble onto it in jungle paths, is insatiable. Its only food is living flesh."

That was the end of the leader's story. Darkness was eliminating the world around us, the Andes had vanished, even the nearby bushes were barely clutching shreds of their reality. We could see quite large bats wheeling on the edges of extinction. The leader squinted rapidly at us, tears flooding the outer deltas of his eyes. He slid a Mickey of whisky from the pea-jacket under his sou'wester, unscrewing the cap with unerring left hand whilst lifting the bottle to his open mouth with his right.

In spite of his own popularity, the leader's narrative did not please all of those assembled in their dripping oilskins around that roaring Patagonian fire. Some of these men who would rise next morning to pursue the last living mylodon criticized the story for its lack of relevance to their situation in Patagonia. They demanded realism, not the kind of primitivist fantasy they detected all too often for their tastes, they said, in the leader's stories. Not the cook, however, with his scraggy red beard and flaking skin. He praised the story's "organic structure, its thematic integrity, and its attention to the unities of time and place." No one else was willing to go that far, but there was general acknowledgement of the requisite element of sadness in the story. The discussion was all very revealing, all very useful.

Johnny Chips, ship's carpenter and expedition handyman, had a sad story to tell. He rocked back and forth on a small barrel, which, because of his weight (he was a heavy man) had already hollowed a smooth indentation in the wet, reddish earth beneath him. For all his drooping moustache and long face, Chips had seen us through hard times — many a lifelike female miniature he had carved for the comfort of the lonely men before the mast on a long voyage.

He himself, however, was above everything a scholar, his cabin stowed to the gunwales with books that took precedence over his carpenter's tools. He always kept his nose covered with a little black leather cone tied behind his head with black shoelaces. When he was telling a story, his eyes would become unstable, strobing wildly in time with his words. The rasp of the wood file was in his voice:

"Thomas à Kempis was a medieval Dutchman who never went to sea, who never knew of Patagonia's existence. He was the man who wrote *Imitatio Christi*, known to us as *The Imitation of Christ*.

"He lived out his long life and died in due course, everyone agreeing that he was the holiest man of the age. Soon, miracles began happening around his grave: missing legs and arms sprouted back, eyesight and hearing were restored. He was especially good with piles and syphilis — decayed noses would grow on again."

The men around the fire did not doubt that the plight of Chips's own nose was the result of a carpentry accident long ago, as he had often assured them.

"Because of the miracles, the Church set out to make Thomas à Kempis a saint, they didn't begrudge him that. They delegated a team of specialists led by a cardinal to see to the exhumation of his body six months after his death as part of the canonizing procedure. The body would have to be completely uncorrupted to satisfy them. Even better if it had a very nice smell coming from it, a sure sign that the man buried there was a saint.

"On the day of the exhumation, a wet wintry day, a big crowd gathered, it being a Saturday afternoon, and not much else going on. Some of the people who claimed Thomas à Kempis had cured them (along with the usual quota of phonies) took the occasion to show off their shiny new eyes, or lily-white legs (no one seems to have received teeth, the most frequently requested and most rarely granted miracle in those days and since, according to researchers). The grave-diggers started shovelling the heavy earth, and after they had penetrated the topsoil, the most aromatic of smells filled all the air of that graveyard, sweeter than any rose, or even any tulip they had ever smelt.

"Then, bump! The long-handled shovels clanged against the coffin! The diggers looped ropes around it and a gang of workmen jerked it up to the surface, all sheathed in lead, the damp clay sticking to it. It had been in that hole, by then, almost seven months.

"The cardinal ordered the soldiers to keep the crowd back. The coffin was laid out on trestles, and one of the team began to jimmy off the lid. The people were hushed now, though some of them were already praying quietly to Thomas à Kempis, hoping to impress the saint-to-be with their confidence.

"The lid squealed ajar. The cardinal and his team moved closer to have a good look at the disinterred saint. 'Oh Christ!' shouted the cardinal, cowering back at what he saw inside that half-open coffin.

"He saw that the interior of the lid of the coffin was grooved with deep scratches. That Thomas à Kempis's dead face was indeed perfectly preserved, but his eyes were bulged open. That his fingers were curled like the claws of a vulture and his fingernails were all broken with wooden splinters to the quick. That his winding sheet was stained around his middle with urine and excrement.

"Poor Thomas à Kempis. The cardinal who had witnessed the opening of the coffins of hundreds of candidates for sainthood understood. The body had not been fully dead when they buried him, but had been in a deep coma. Who could know when he woke up out of it and into his nightmare? One of the men who had been at the funeral half a year before said he was sure he had heard noises from the coffin on that day, but was afraid it was the devil's work.

"Well. That was it for Thomas à Kempis. The cardinal ordered the coffin closed and put back in the earth. No one needed to be told that Thomas couldn't be made a saint, for what curses might he not have howled in that narrow coffin? The scratches told everything. Wouldn't a real saint have been content with his fate, even if he had been buried a little too early?

"No. That was it for Thomas à Kempis. His book was marvellous, the whole world agreed. But the author was only human after all."

Chips rocked gently on his barrel, his eyes resuming their usual orbits. His story was over.

The rain fell a little more heavily now in Patagonia, and even the bushes near the fire had lost their battle with the night.

Debate immediately began over Chips's story. Some of the men were indignant over the way Thomas à Kempis had been treated, and insisted that anyone in their right minds would try to get out of a coffin if they'd been buried alive. The case only reconfirmed their worst suspicions about institutions and regulations generally. Chips rocked gently on his barrel.

One of the men objected to the *way* in which Chips told the story.

He charged that, in deliberately delaying the final revelation for so long, Chips had indulged in the most hackneyed of attention-holding devices. The leader himself came to life at this point. He disengaged himself a moment from his bottle to argue that Chips ought to have begun with the ending, rather than toying with their feelings in what the leader, now weeping helplessly, considered to be a heartless fashion, and one that he himself would never have used. Chips refused to be baited.

Some men quibbled over the historical factuality of the story: in their minds, Chips ought to have made it clear right from the start that he was dealing in speculation, at best, and certainly not in history. This criticism startled one of the little cabin-boys, a great favourite of Chips, who had been allowed to stay up late. He said that Chips was always telling him such stories about historical figures, and that he'd never doubted their truth. On hearing this, a few of the men reckoned Chips ought to be ashamed of himself.

The cook, however, had been biding his time. His red beard challenged all opposition. He congratulated Chips on "his refusal to be intimidated by history," and praised him for "the intransigent penetration of his metaphor."

This comment effectively ended the discussion.

Chips rocked backwards and forwards on his barrel, backwards into the flickering darkness, forwards into the light of the blazing fire, and said nothing, nothing at all. Just smiling, in that damp Patagonian night, the tense smile of a man not given to smiling.

Hundreds of bats, it seemed, were now swooping in and out of the firelight above us. The leader pulled out his pocket-watch and dangled it in the light. He yawned.

"Time for one more," he said.

We all turned towards the chief engineer. He was a man from the islands, who would occasionally take over medical duties when the ship's doctor was ill (an illness brought on by whisky). The chief's hands were familiar with bunker oil and heavy steel piping, yet he had the elegant fingers of a pianist or a surgeon, the milky blue eyes of a dreamer. He spoke into the silence:

"A thing happened in my home town when I was a young boy. A new doctor with a strong foreign accent came up to practice at our end of the island, bringing his wife and four children, two boys and two girls all under ten years of age. The man was thin with a head like a snake. The wife was beautiful.

"After only a month, the thing happened. On a sunny September morning, this new doctor stumbled through the door of the police station looking very upset, and said that his wife was missing, having gone for her daily walk the day before and not come back. He had looked everywhere.

"The police made sure she had not boarded the ferry for the mainland, then organized a search for her. They searched day and night for two days, but there was no sign of her.

"The children showed up at school as usual. They did not look well, they were all pale and washed out as though they had been crying. What was most noticeable was the way they walked. All of them walked the stiff walk of an old man.

"The island children did not know them well, and were shy about asking what was the matter, thinking it must have something to do with their mother's disappearance.

"But on their second day back at school, one of the little girls, who was six years old, turned very sick and fell over from her desk onto the floor in convulsions, holding her stomach.

"The old schoolmistress made her comfortable in the staff room with blankets and a pillow and phoned her father, the doctor, to come right away.

"The little girl kept on groaning in agony, and the schoolmistress tried to coax her to show where the pain was. The little girl was not willing at first, but she was in pain and saw the schoolmistress wanted to help. So she began to unbutton her dress. But her father, the doctor, came rushing into the staff room shouting, 'No! No!' and lifted her away in his arms out into his car. He then came back for the other three children, and took them all away with him.

"But the old schoolmistress had seen enough, and phoned the police station.

"Without any delay, the sergeant and his constable drove to the doctor's house on the cliffs overlooking the ocean. They knocked, and had to wait a few minutes before the doctor, looking nervous, came to the door. The sergeant said he'd like to look at the children. The doctor at first said they were too sick to be disturbed, but had to let them in.

"All the children were lying in their beds in one large room on the ocean side of the house and anyone could see how sick they were. The sergeant knew what he had to do. He asked them to open up their clothing for him. They all did so, with groans and gasps of pain.

"He understood the reason for their suffering.

"The sergeant saw that each of those four children had a large incision along the centre of their abdomens, the sutures fresh, the wounds inflamed.

"Their father, the doctor, stood watching all of this, sobbing loudly. When the sergeant asked him why the children had been operated upon, he would say nothing.

"The sergeant took all four children to the hospital at the other end of the island.

"The resident surgeon there, a kind man, saw the sergeant's concern, and ordered the little girl who had been in the greatest pain to be taken into the operating theatre where he was about to conduct a class in pathology for some nurses. The little girl was anaesthetized, and the resident showed the nurses how pus mixed with the blood was oozing from the wound. No wonder she had been in agony.

"The resident then cut the sutures and lifted them away. He slid his fingers into the wound and groped around. He said he could feel a lump of some sort. He managed to grip part of it with his calipers, and carefully fished it out, holding it up in the air.

"All of those assembled round that table saw something they would never forget. The resident had snared in the calipers a severed human hand, dripping blood and pus. He was holding it by its thumb, and they could all see, quite clearly, the gold wedding ring on its middle finger, and the scarlet polish on the long fingernails."

No one stirred around that camp-fire in Patagonia. The night had turned chilly, the members of the expedition crouched nearer to the fire's heat. The chief engineer continued:

"That was how they found out that the new doctor had killed his wife. He had cut off parts of her and buried them inside the children. Each of the four children contained a foot or a hand. Later, the family pets, a Highland collie and a big ginger cat, were found lying in the house cellar, half alive. They too had abdominal incisions. The local veterinarian discovered the woman's eyes in the dog and her ears in the cat.

"The resident testified later that he hoped never to perform such a salvage operation again. He was sure that if the man had had enough children and pets, he'd have managed to conceal every part of her. As it was they found the rest of her body under some rocks by the shore.

"The resident said the father's workmanship was a marvel, he had never seen such skill. The murderer himself was silent. He was later sentenced to death, though his children pleaded for his life. The islanders would never allow hangings on the island for fear of bad luck. They did not object, however, to his being hanged on the mainland."

The chief engineer's story was ended. The Patagonian darkness silenced the men for a while. Then Chips, rocking smoothly on his barrel, said in his grating voice that he thought the story was well enough done, but that it was disgusting rather than sad, and therefore not really suitable to the occasion.

The cook rarely liked the chief's stories. He could hardly wait, his scraggy beard bristling, to denounce this one as "another rather boring instance of the metaphysical/erotic struggle for authenticity and freedom in daily life, and of the problems of coping with the dichotomy of the Word/word, its abstract and concrete dimensions in experience and language."

No one seemed enthusiastic about pursuing this particular line of analysis.

One of the men, a friend of the chief, tried to be diplomatic, suggesting that perhaps the story should be understood symbolically rather than literally. He doubted, anyway, that the human body could be used as a repository of dead limbs.

The chief engineer answered this last objection, and all objections in a very simple manner. He rose to his feet in the Patagonian night before the smouldering fire, and pulled the front of his shirt up from his waist. There, just above the waistline, we could all see a long horizontal scar, a white corrugation about nine inches long dissecting his pale, northern skin.

That seemed to settle everything. The leader, a man of habit, never commented on the final story of an evening. Yet his tearful eyes told all. A man of habit, he yawned, nevertheless, his ritual last yawn, his mouth bracketed by flowing tears, and he stood up.

"Time to turn in," he said. "Tomorrow morning bright and early it will be our task to ensnare the last mylodon on this earth."

Without reluctance, we all arose now, drowsy with pleasure at the sadness of the world, anticipating the warmth of sleeping bags, the shelter of canvas against the rain which whispered noisily to the failing logs. Soon the fire would be dead, and the darkness would extinguish us all, here in Patagonia.

Eckhardt at a Window

Eckhardt at a Window

The dusty wooden frame of the window holds nine double-glazed panes of glass, three levels of three panes on top of each other. If Inspector Eckhardt stands on tiptoe on the threadbare carpet, the top panes are at his eye level. The middle row is comfortably situated for him, for he is a man of medium height. He has to stoop slightly, however, his chin on the sill, to look through the bottom row. If he stands a few feet away, the window is all one greater window, the panes look symmetrical, crystalline, even identical. But from close up, at nose distance, which he prefers, each pane is individual, unique, each discloses new worlds to Inspector Eckhardt's eye. A bevel in the double glass here, a warp there, reveal the reflections of twin, overlapping grotesque faces in two grotesque rooms, Chinese boxes that do not quite fit. As for what he sees on the outside — a warp in the pane, a bubble, a bevel, invent a city he can scarcely recognize of monstrous trees and nightmare houses reshaping themselves constantly as he moves his grey head, a landscape of plastic writhing forever in an inferno.

Inspector Eckhardt is thinking about the deaths, one year ago, of a woman and a man. He remembers the tall, beautiful, fair-haired woman he first met on that dull, November day, in this northern city. She was shivering, wearing a thin dress under a short coat. Her face was oval, a noticeable nose, green, green eyes. The lower lids were convex, half-eclipsing those two green worlds.

Inspector Eckhardt, a widower without children, a meditative man, liked the look of her right away, her voice, an innocence about her. She was long-legged, long-striding in spite of her grief — she had come to the old police station to report a death. In her deep, surprising voice, she wanted to tell him about the ludicrous accident that had happened less than an hour before. Her strange eyelids could not stop the tears from spilling out.

She was apologetic, but not about her grief. She was sorry for this: that in her confusion, she hadn't paid much attention to the location of the house where the accident had happened. It had no telephone, so she ran outside, along the street till she found a taxi, and asked for the nearest police station. And now, where was the house with the dead body? She was sure of one thing only: it was on a tree-lined street, maybe a mile or two away.

The Inspector smiled at her insistence on this fact. He did not tell her that the entire district for miles around the station was full of tree-lined streets, that it was a forest masquerading as a city. People who had lived here a long time knew their way around, knew how to see the differences between one street of trees and another. His new men often lost their way the first few times out.

Darkness was sinking in as she talked, sitting in the wooden chair in front of his desk. Through the window behind her, Inspector Eckhardt could see those very streets beginning to fade into night. It was a cold November darkness, and the lamps would hardly illumine those streets, making it useless to go looking for the house. She didn't know, in fact she said she'd never known, even the number of the house, or the name of the street. He told her, as kindly as he could, that it didn't matter much. Her friend, being dead, would be content to wait till the morning.

She shuddered. Yet she wanted to talk, and he wanted to listen to her, to watch the movement of those strange eyes, as much because of the pleasure it gave him as to help her ease herself of her burden of sorrow. He told her a formal statement could wait till the morning, but that he'd like to hear all about her friend. She should just relax and say whatever came to mind.

"A little spout of blood." She used that phrase several times. She said this little spout of blood, just a drop or two, used to spurt from her friend's forehead right between his eyebrows at least once a day. Surely that would be remarkable in anyone. The blood would trickle down his face, and he'd wipe it with a Kleenex, nervously, a horse flicking at flies. She wasn't long up from the country, and had been sitting in a bar, when he picked her up a month ago. She lik-ed the look of him, and said nothing even when she first saw the blood spout. It used to frighten her, and it would fill him with a devastating sadness. But she said nothing.

She found out, eventually, why the blood made him so sad. One day they were sitting, talking. He was stroking, as usual, the crystal of his digital watch as he talked, intent on the nervous transforma-tions of the little figures under the glass. He looked up and stared into her eyes. He was afraid, he said, that the blood that spouted out of his forehead wasn't his own. It was the blood of all the people he'd killed gushing back out of him.

Killings. He saw how shocked she was, and so he began telling her about them.

When he used to kill, he said, he felt as though he was watching someone else do it, a creature who looked like him, but who was on the other side of a two-way mirror. Years ago, when he was a child, he used to think it must be some other child who looked like him burying cats alive or setting them alight with gasoline, watching them try to leap out of their pain, living Catherine wheels. Then, years later, surely that was some other young boy who just happen-ed to look like him, pushing another lonely boy into a disused canal, standing there, fascinated by the muddy gurgles, and the eventual brown calm. Or shoulder-charging an old man, light as a feather, down the dark stairwell of an apartment building and watching him crumple silently at the bottom, a broken butterfly with blood at the mouth. And even now, he could hardly admit that this killer was no one else but himself, this brown-bearded man who killed for hire and showed no pity for any of those he destroyed with his gun, his knife, his car, by fire, by water, or by other necessary means.

But one night as he was getting ready for bed, the blood gushed, for the first time, out of his head. He was undressing in front of the mirror, trying to comprehend the man on the other side of the glass, when it erupted. He quickly wiped it away, already fearful, and saw that there was no sign of a cut, not even a burst pimple, only the smooth forehead of a killer.

It wasn't long after, one night in a bar, that he met her, and they became lovers, he loving someone, and that, too, for the first time in his life.

He told her he felt he was divided once more into separate parts by meeting her. She'd somehow built a transparent wall around him, so that now his past life was someone else's, an unloved man he hardly knew.

He wanted to dedicate himself now to loving, the way he had before to killing. He wondered if love could cancel out, somehow, all of the deaths. So he began taking her to the places where he'd done his murders over the years, and they made love standing up in alleys and hallways, lying down in city parks and seedy basements, in daytime and in the night. Always, in spite of everything, the blood came.

Then, just that day, they went to a house in a tree-lined street. He'd phoned her early in the afternoon, and they'd taken a taxi to the house.

They went straight upstairs, she hardly noticing the creaky stairs, the faded prints in their cracked frames on the walls, to a dusty room with some shabby chairs and a rusted wall-mirror. In the middle of the bare floor stood a metal-framed coffee table with a glass top.

They made love in front of the mirror. She watched his hands move under her clothing in the reflection: the image of the two lovers in the mirror before her, and the feel of his hands on her flesh doubled her pleasure.

After the love-making, he'd sent her downstairs to the kitchen to make coffee. She was standing by the stove when she heard a crash upstairs. She called up to him from the hall to ask if anything was wrong. She thought he called back that it was okay, so she went into the kitchen again.

After a few minutes, a drip fell past her head onto the chipped white stove, a reddish splotch. And another. For a moment she didn't understand. She looked up at the ceiling where a reddish-brown drip was gathering. She knew then what it was.

Terrified, she ran out of the kitchen and up the stairs, her feet hollow on the worn linoleum, hardly noticing the faded prints of hunting scenes behind broken glass. She reached the landing and looked through the open living-room door.

The bearded man is spread-eagled across the frame of a low coffee-table whose glass top has collapsed. He himself is impaled upon a sliver of green glass about eighteen inches long. It has pierced his back, travelling on through his body inside the left shoulder-blade, driven by his weight, slicing through his heart like a butcher's knife.

The point of the glass protrudes through his chest without tearing his green silk shirt, but far enough to make an obscene bosom. His eyes are open and he looks surprised. In the middle of his forehead, a little ruby of wet blood is forming.

She runs to him, sobbing. He is quite, quite dead.

He must have sat right down on the glass-topped table, making it cave in, explode at the weight of him. It was meant to take a vase of flowers, or a glossy picture book, never a man's weight. He must have fallen backward into the empty frame, crucifying himself, skewered by a long sliver wedged against the floor, his body making new lips to suck in the glass.

Inspector Eckhardt felt sorry for her. Her green eyes were full of tears, this tall, fair-haired woman, occasionally touching his arm as she talked. She still couldn't believe what had happened. For so long she too had been alone, sad. Then she met the bearded man and her life was full of meaning, love became a barricade against an unbearable past. And now the barrier had been demolished.

She looked tired now. The Inspector nodded in sympathy. He didn't even know her name, but that could wait. Nor did she call the bearded man any name at all. Always it was "he," with a little emphasis. Inspector Eckhardt wondered if she even knew the man's name, but he didn't ask. He'd enjoyed listening to her, and he could get all the details from her tomorrow morning.

He told her she could go home now and come back in the

morning early to make a statement and help them find the house. Again, her strange green eyes filled. She said she'd no place to go, she'd given up her apartment just that day, so that she could move in with the bearded man.

Inspector Eckhardt looked at her, liking the looks of her, tall and warm. He liked the way she would reach out across the desk and touch his arm quite unselfconsciously, trusting him.

It was no problem, he said. She could stay in the station's little night-shift room. He'd ask the duty sergeant to get her a cup of coffee and a sandwich. She should try to sleep, even though it was early, because next morning she'd have to help them find the house with the body of her dead lover.

After she left with the sergeant, the Inspector sat for a while, thinking about her, and the strange accident she'd come to report. He thought, too, about his own mood of contentment, that he'd be seeing her again in the morning. He couldn't help feeling that in some way he wasn't yet sure of, this was a remarkable day for him.

Inspector Eckhardt did indeed see her very early the next morning. The fair-haired woman must have slipped out of the station during the night, and when he saw her in the early morning, there was a great change in her condition.

Dawn is just breaking, a frosty November dawn in the city. The sky is a heavy sheet of opaque glass with fissures prised apart by wedges of sunlight.

On a piece of waste ground stands a huddle of men, their breath silently trumpeting in front of them. A car pulls up on the nearby street, the engine throbbing, and a grey-haired, older man in a heavy winter coat picks his way through the sparkling weeds towards the men.

"Over here, Inspector Eckhardt."

The Inspector nods to the men, and leans forwards to look at the shape lying on the iron ground. He can see that it is the frozen body of a long-legged young woman in a skimpy dress, her clothes, her fair hair sculpted in hoar-frost, a sparkling Christmas bundle. She is sprawled on her back. Her eyes are the eyes of a statue, completely whitened in the frost of this November morning.

Inspector Eckhardt also sees, glittering in the occasional sunshine, the long splinter of frosted glass protruding from her belly, a lethal banner which she grips in her two frozen hands.

Inspector Eckhardt was too shocked by this death, too saddened by the thought that he'd never see the woman again. He knew he must work, and work, and work. The investigation of her death wasn't in his hands; it was his job to find the body of the bearded man, and he'd waste no time that day in getting on with it.

He and his team knocked on door after door, peered through dozens of dusty windows, examined every house that seemed unoccupied in those tree-lined streets. In vain. Some of Inspector Eckhardt's men wondered out loud whether, perhaps, her story was just a bit far-fetched. Late in the afternoon, he himself began to probe the fringes of that possibility: that there was no body, that she had made up an insane lie.

Then, just before dusk, news came in that the body had been found.

The house is on one of those tree-lined streets in the maze of tree-lined streets surrounding the station. The streets are mirror images of each other. Only a bump on the road here, an oddity in architecture there makes the difference to those who know.

The grey-haired man steps out of the cruiser and walks up the pathway of a small, run-down house. The door opens, and staleness makes a brief raid on the sharp, colder outside air. He notes the creaky stairs, the faded prints on the wall, the worn linoleum. On the dim landing, he glimpses three rooms: a bathroom with a chipped sink, an empty bedroom with a cracked mirror on the wall. Then the living-room, with another smell, one he knows only too well.

"Right in here, Inspector Eckhardt."

Through the parasitic fuss of photographers and detectives, the Inspector sees, by the light of a bare ceiling bulb, the dead man, crucified on a rectangular metal frame, broken glass all around him, his eyes wide open. His face is bearded, a thin brown beard on a thin face, his hairline receding. It is the face of a young man who has never been young. His cheeks are lined with experience and sadness.

But two things are ominously wrong. No gush of blood stains the

dead forehead, one of the last things she had told him. The bearded man's brow is smooth and unmarked. But more disturbing still,
he has not been pierced through his back. Instead, Inspector
Eckhardt can see, as can all the others, the broad end of a long
sliver of glass protruding sickly from between his legs, an obscene
phallus coated in blood and excrement.

That was all a year ago, a year in which no resolution to the mystery
of the deaths had appeared. Inspector Eckhardt had made sure the
investigation of the fair-haired woman's death was pursued without
slacking. But no witness could be found, no motive appeared. Her
past was a blank, no one claimed her or identified her. The in-
vestigators dealt with her death as a murder, but they did concede
that it was just possible she might have stabbed herself with the
shard of glass — a very unpleasant way to commit suicide.

As for the bearded man impaled on the glass, nothing could be
discovered about him except that he had just recently paid a year's
rent on the old house on the tree-lined street.

Inspector Eckhardt remembered how she said they'd always
make love on the scene of former killings. So, day after day he
wearied his eyes with the dust and faded type of old files. He even
began having nightmares about seedy crimes camouflaged by the
trees of those streets. But he could find no record of a killing in that
house. It belonged to an old couple who had retired and migrated
to the South.

Soon the entire case of the fair-haired woman and the bearded
man was interred, in its turn, in a filing cabinet. Inspector
Eckhardt's superiors told him plainly that the two deaths, no matter how strange, of an apprentice hooker and a presumed lover-
cum-hired-killer were of minor importance in the general scheme
of things.

But Inspector Eckhardt did not forget, could not forget. For him,
he didn't quite know why, the case was of major importance in his
"general scheme of things." He'd stand for hours looking out of his
window, a juggler with too many rubber balls, trying just once to
put it all together. He was beginning to consider that his career up

to that point had been a time of innocence, a novitiate. He felt that he too had walked right through a mirror, and everything was changed.

The case, he had to admit to himself, delighted him as much as it puzzled him with its possibilities, its enigmas. Yes, she was dead. But now he was high priest of his own private religion, and must create a theology around the mysteries. Part of his ritual was to meditate daily upon the fair-haired woman, at times his goddess, at times a demon. Why had the description she'd given of the death of the bearded man been so accurate yet so wrong? How could the dead man have answered her call from the kitchen? Why had she left the police station during the night? What had made her go to the waste ground to die?

Daily, he invents ingenious resolutions to the mystery. For example, he theorizes, keeping the details sketchy, that it could be a murder-suicide. The essence is this: the fair-haired woman must murder the bearded man by somehow (this is one of the very vague parts) forcing him to sit on the fragment of glass in the old house, then she must slip away to the waste ground to stab herself in the stomach.

Or, in another version, it is the bearded man who must be the murderer. He must go to the waste ground to meet the fair-haired woman, stab her in the stomach with the piece of glass, then return to that musty house and sit down, quite deliberately, on the sliver of glass.

Naturally, in this second version of the murder-suicide theory, the order of the deaths is reversed. But then, neither first nor second version accounts for her visit to the police-station, nor for her determination to tell her story. Yet the Inspector finds something satisfying in both versions, maybe the suggestion of a doomed, perverted love, maybe the symbolism of the glass. Or maybe, it's just the enigma of which of the two is the murderer, which the suicide.

Inspector Eckhardt is also gently nursing a double-murder theory. It goes like this: someone wants to kill the fair-haired woman and the bearded man, perhaps to avenge one of his paid killings — the motive is unclear. The murderer somehow forces the bearded man to sit on the sliver of glass (again, the Inspector is unhappy with this part), somehow terrifies the fair-haired woman into lying convincingly to the police (slightly less difficult for the Inspector to imagine), and then into leaving the station in the middle of the night for the waste ground, to meet her own murderer (tricky, this part too, the Inspector admits).

Sometimes the Inspector even proposes two separate murderers, one for the bearded man, one for the girl, perhaps acting in collusion, perhaps not, although the use of the glass is so unusual it suggests a conspiracy. The flexibility of the two-murderer theory, however, is its main appeal: the permutations of which-killer-kills-whom-and-why are expanded marvellously by this simple ploy.

Inspector Eckhardt likes all variations of the double-murder theory for another reason. They exonerate the fair-haired woman, making her perhaps the tragic victim of her love for a felon. Besides, the slaying of the bearded man, an admitted assassin, is reassuring for the Inspector: justice, no matter how rough, still prowls the streets of the city.

But one thing always bothers him. Why, he constantly asks himself, did the fair-haired woman come to the station and lie? That, he still finds hardest of all to take.

For a year, Inspector Eckhardt speculated and speculated, enjoyed speculating, standing there by his window. He never lost patience at the incompleteness of his theories, for he felt confident that, in time, the whorls, the distortions, the bumps would disappear, and the clear, inevitable truth would stand forth.

Then, just that morning, almost a year to the day after the deaths, he was obliged to look at the whole matter differently. Not a mile from the station, a crew of hydro-company men had been making routine inspections of the lines. They had been checking out an old house when they found something grisly.

The grey-haired man, stocky in his winter coat, swings his legs out of the cruiser. He walks along the path to the door of the house where some men in hard hats stand smoking and talking. It's a small house, paint peeling from the clapboard. This house would be hard to distinguish from most of the others in the tree-lined street.

He pushes open the creaky door, ducking past a brief ambush by the stale air, and walks along the hallway to the staircase — he can hear the sound of voices upstairs. He climbs the creaking staircase with its worn linoleum, his shoes echoing. He notes the faded prints on the walls. He stops on the landing, where the smell is even mustier. In a room with an open door, a few men are scuttling around, maggots in uniform.

"Come in, Inspector Eckhardt," one of them says, without turning. And he sees what occupies their attention.

The fully-clothed body of a man lies on its back in the metal frame of a glass-topped coffee-table surrounded by broken glass. The body has lain there a long time. The Inspector can see that the face and the exposed parts of the flesh have turned a mottled blue. The cheeks have partly decomposed, exposing the bone. The eyes have dried up to raisins. The clothing and the floor beneath the skeletal frame of the table are heavily stained by the leakage of body fluids.

The cause of death is very clear: the body has been pierced through the back by a long sliver of glass, wedged against the floor. The glass has penetrated so deeply that the point, a deadly nipple, sticks out of the chest through the material of what was once a light green shirt.

Lying on the button band of the shirt, a rag of brown hair has peeled away from the chin. A scalp of long brown hair hangs from the back of the lolling head like a trophy. The ends of the fingers have decomposed, exposing bone, but on the mottled blue left wrist, a digital watch dangles. The angular numbers are still prowling agitatedly under their glass cover.

Inspector Eckhardt, back in his office in the station, stands by his window, late in the afternoon. He is thinking of the fair-haired girl, the bearded men, and the possibility of faceless, shadowy avengers. In the window panes, he fancies he sees them, playing a variety of parts, here stabbing themselves, there stabbing each other, or each being stabbed by all the others in a frenzy of glass.

The Inspector sighs. The darkness outside is deepening, and

soon he will see with cockroach eyes the multiple images of himself reflected more distinctly in the window. Vaguely, through the double glaze, the nightscape of the city will emerge on this November afternoon, creating itself in light, the beginnings of a miraculous painting-by-numbers.

Inspector Eckhardt, standing by his window, is not discontented with the way things have worked out. He knows now that he has no wish ever to solve his mystery (he feels sure that it *is* his, meant for him alone), only to contemplate it, to delight in its complexities.

He walks slowly back to his desk marvelling again at the discovery of the second bearded man's body. Behind him, nine, or is it eighteen, other misshapen Inspector Eckhardts slide, hobble, somersault back to their separate desks. They sit down in unison. After a moment's pause, as on a signal given, all of them, with the most convoluted motions, reach for pencils, find them with an impossible accuracy, and begin to write.

The One-Legged Men

The One-Legged Men

You're on their ground now. Don't be fooled by their looks. Watch out for the following: abnormal frequency of stumbling over kerbs and doorsteps, studied balance in walking, reliance upon arm-strength in getting up out of chairs, stiffness in lower limbs, hesitancy in picking up dropped things. A sure sign is one sharp crease and one dull in a pair of trousers. You can often go by shoes: in a suspect pair, each will seem well used, but one of them not by any natural foot. Remember this: whenever you note great anima-tion and expressiveness in conversation by the use of hands and upper body, you're probably on to something.

From "A Description of Muirton," James R. Ross, Ayrshire Today *(Glasgow, 1950)*

Muirton, East Ayrshire, nestles in a treeless valley beyond which the Lead Hills stutter towards the Border with England. It is one of those villages that cluster around a coal-mine. The mine itself looks, to the visitor, like a suppuration from the bare, but otherwise healthy flesh of the timeless moorlands. Yet, in the usual paradoxical way, the huge slag-heaps of these ugly mines that abound in this part of Ayrshire may also be likened to breasts that nourish a breed of men and women capable of great physical tenacity and intellectual vigour. Like the scrawny heather that grows all around, these people have their seasons of beauty.

The boys of Muirton don't like school. The boys of Muirton don't like poetry. The boys of Muirton do like: playing soccer; trout-fishing; pitch-and-toss. So far as talking goes, they like: talking about girls; talking about getting a job in the mine when they're fifteen. The six-times-a-day hoot of the mine's siren is like the Pied Piper's tune to them. It calls, coaxes, cajoles them into an exclusive abyss.

From Annals of the Modern Ayrshire Parish, *Rev. James O'Connell (Dumfries, 1979)*
The day that brought Muirton fame for its excess of one-legged inhabitants occurred during my first year as minister there. It was a day not blessed in its beginnings so far as weather was concerned. A murky morning carried the threat of rain — the Lead Hills, so appropriately named, in my view, were hidden in mist — even though summer had ostensibly begun. June in Muirton, I was to learn, is only slightly warmer than January. The day-shift workers, many of whom were my parishioners, set out along the shrub-lined roadway to the mine at about six o'clock. There were fathers, sons, uncles, nephews, cousins, in truth "by the dozens." On their way, they passed the homeward-bound night-shift workers, all black-faced, even the young boys — God bless them — bound for dinner and bed, their world topsy-turvy. No one, of course, had any premonition of the trial some of them were to undergo that very day in fulfilling the mysterious will of their Maker.

The men and boys of Muirton. They stand in clusters at the gates of the mine elevator. The gloomy tower creaks eerily above them. A giant Ferris wheel. They await the daily, commonplace, infernal descent.

From Coalminer to Honourable Member, *Tom Kennedy, MP (Glasgow, 1946)*

The first few times you went down in the cage it scared the wits out of you. Your stomach never seemed to get back to its usual place. Some of the new boys used to wet their trousers and everybody would make wisecracks about the poor lads for many weeks afterwards. But we all got used to the cage eventually, and most of the time it never crossed your mind how far down you were going — 1,000 or 10,000 feet, it didn't make any difference. As you went deeper, the air used to get warmer. Even in the middle of winter, the sweat would be lashing off you.

What I miss now — I wish we had some of it here in the House of Commons — is the great spirit we used to have in those days.

This one jokes, this one laughs, this one yawns, this one spits, this one whistles, this one day-dreams, this one scratches his neck, this one turns his head and looks up to the shroud of hills. The final squad entering the cage.

From The Ayr Daily News, *July 4*
MUIRTON HORROR UPDATE

No one knows yet for sure how the disaster happened that shook this little Ayrshire town yesterday morning. One thing is certain, hardly a family has been spared.

Experts from the National Coal Board are examining at this very instant the wrecked elevator cage at the bottom of the shaft to determine why the braking mechanism failed. They expect to have a report ready for next month's Inquiry. However, they reconstruct the tragedy as follows:

At approximately 6:40 A.M., forty men and boys, the final day-shift squad, entered the cage for their descent to the coal face. Some time in the next few minutes as the cage descended to the 4,000 feet level, they would hear the alarm bell and see the flashing red light, warning them that the cage was out of control.

At this point they would take the normal precautionary

measures. Inspector David McCann, 54, of the Miners' Safety Board, describes these: "The miners are drilled once a week in safety procedures. In the case of a cage going out of control they all know what to do. They have to reach up and grasp firmly one of the leather hand-straps attached to the roof of the cage. Then they lift one leg off the floor.

"In this way, with any luck, depending on how far the cage has to fall, they might save one leg when they hit the bottom even though the cage comes down quite hard."

This afternoon I met two of the rescue team who were present when the smashed cage was opened. They were, Orderly John McCallum, 43, and Orderly Tom McLeary, 29. McLeary had no comment to make, but McCallum gave me this brief reaction:

"It's the worst thing I've seen in years at this job. It's hard to believe anybody survived it. The cage was all twisted so we had a very hard time with the acetylene torches getting inside it. We could hear noises so we knew some of them were still alive. When we got the front off, it wasn't easy to know what to do, it was such a sight."

It is now established that there were thirteen survivors out of the forty, so it seems that the safety measures worked in part. At the point of impact, the leather handstraps absorbed some of the shock, but then snapped — that was to be expected. The rest of the body-weight was then transferred completely to the supporting leg. That leg was smashed immediately to pulp.

The Jury is Out. The Jury is In. Boards of Inquiry, Commissions of Inquiry, Industrial Tribunals, Insurance Adjustments, Compensation Committees, Medical Examinations, Burdens of Proof, Amendments to Safety Subsections, Revised Regulations, Compulsory Hard Hats.

From "Your Letters," The Edinburgh Times, *November 6*
Sir,
I would like to add some pertinent data to your recent correspondence on the issue of the physiological appearance of

any part of the human anatomy upon its being smashed to a pulp.

As one of the physicians who examined the victims of the recent Muirton disaster, I feel qualified to comment with some authority upon the effects on the lower limbs of what is now called "the pulping phenomenon."

I would like, first, to dispel the speculative notion that pulped limbs after a massive fall look, as one of your correspondents hypothesised, "like minced beef à la Sweeney Todd." Nonsense. Aside from the inordinate amount of blood on the cage floor at Muirton, the signs were much less obvious.

Let us consider for example the pulped limbs of the thirteen survivors. It appears that at the moment of impact, the femur, patella, tibia, and fibula disintegrated, though, in one case, the femur was pushed up into the lower intestinal tract causing severe, but not fatal injury.

But, after the disintegration of the bones, the limbs appear to have sprung back into their accustomed positions with skin and muscle seemingly intact. At first glance, therefore, it was impossible to assess the damage. It was when the Orderlies tried to move the bodies they discovered that they were attempting to lift limbs that were completely gelid. Immediate amputation was, of course, absolutely necessary.

I might add that, in the cases of the dead miners, one or both legs of each had been similarly traumatised. Why death resulted instantly in their cases, even though their upper bodies remained quite functional, is worthy, surely, of some research.

I trust these remarks will be of help in settling the issue,

Sincerely,
J. Blair, MD

Tell me, do you know? can you say? would you mind? could you try? got the message? get the picture? walking on four feet, and two feet, and one foot, and three feet, the fearful, fearful beast.

Bits and Pieces, Odds and Ends
1. A survivor, one year later: "I'm going to carry on living in

Muirton. At least when I'm here, people don't look at me as if I'm a freak."

2. A Muirton children's skipping song:

> Skip me one,
> Skip me two,
> Tell me what does your daddy do?
> He lies in his bed,
> And eats fried egg,
> Because he's only got one leg.

3. Stephen Neil, Headmaster of Muirton Primary School: "I know the families of most of the survivors. I get the impression that some of the men and boys have never recovered: they're under psychiatric care for constant nightmares and depression. And impotence."

4. A survivor, one year later: "Did you ever hear tell that a drowning man is supposed to see his whole life passing before him? I often say to the wife that's what happened to me as we went down. I even saw my grandmother, and she's been dead for twenty years now."

5. A survivor, one year later: "I never thought I'd have to do it. Even when we practised the leg-drill, we all used to laugh, because we thought, 'if we ever have to rely on this we'll know we're dead men.' Big Jock McCutcheon used to say, 'Do they think we're all daft? Standing on one leg like a chicken is no way to die.'"

6. A survivor, one year later: "I couldn't make up my mind which leg to give up."

7. A member of the rescue team: "I think they all hoped they were dead."

Knox Abroad

Knox Abroad

The voyage is over. John Knox stands, sways a little, with Clootie, his cat, on the forest-ragged banks of the river (more like the shore of the ocean), on land at last. It is October, and this is an alien place. He looks around and smiles. Nothing has changed, even after a wilderness of sea. His shoes touch dead leaves, the discreet vomit of the trees. He observes the paralysis of the rocks. The winds still blast down from directly above, threatening to hammer him, like a stake, into the ground, drive him under, bury him alive. Every night of the voyage, he saw (he has seen the same thing for twenty years of nights) the planets and the stars desert, rush centrifugally away into the outer universe, as though fleeing a plague. In the mornings, as always, the sun searched him out, singed his ever-so-delicate grey skin. Again he smiles. Even amongst the trees there is no refuge. He bends over and lightly strokes Clootie's black coat. Together they turn and walk along the beaten path, fade into the forest gloom.

"An etymological footnote on the name *Canada*. John Knox, the founder of Scottish Presbyterianism, was apprehended in 1547 by the French and sentenced to serve as a galley-slave in the French navy. After eighteen months, he escaped. A Breton

legend, however, suggests that before escaping, he served some
months on an exploration ship to New France. This is not
impossible. A less reliable tradition supplies the information
that, many years later, after his return to Scotland, one of his
disciples asked him for his opinion of the New World, which
had now become a refuge for the persecuted. Knox is said to
have replied, 'I *canna dae* wi' it, I *canna dae* wi' it,' thus, albeit
inadvertently, giving the country its name."

M. Gobert, *Mémoires des Ecossais*, (Geneva, 1897)

In the galleys he was supposed to be the slave, but he was master, he
knew it and they knew it. The same on the expedition ship. The
mate lacked the nerve to make him holystone the decks alongside
the others, for fear of his tongue. No ears could endure the
monstrous words (predestination! election! reprobation!) he would
hurl against them. Still, he was no burden: when the barber-
surgeon drowned in a storm, two weeks out of St Malo, Knox took
his place — no one else had the stomach for the job. Though he
loathed the unbearable closeness of other living bodies on the
ship. Give him solitary confinement, a narrow dungeon, and he
would have been more content.

The captain, knowing his prowess as a controversialist, tried
often, on this tedious journey, to entice him to his cabin for dinner,
to dispute on matters theological. Knox spat at him as an idolator
like all the others, and refused the bait.

Knox jettisoned the statue of the Virgin. It was on a Sunday, and
the crew assembled for the weekly statue-kissing, a good-luck ritual.
Knox grabbed the statue from its perch by the mainmast and
hurled it, head over tail, halo of stars over serpent's head, out into
the ocean. Where it sank like a stone. The sacrilege horrified the
French sailors, but they kept their hands off him. He joked to his
cat: "The Queen of the Sea cannae swim, Clootie." But they kept
their hands off him.

Physically, Knox was scrawny. He was an aggressive talker, except
to his cat, Clootie, a black creature, sleek, with wicked eyes. The cat
was a growler, a hisser, and in the minds of the sailors, was Knox's
familiar demon. Knox, too, was a growler, but never growled at
Clootie:

"Well, Clootie, my wee man, did you ever see a country so naked of churches? It won't do. I can already imagine a forest of steeples along this river-bank. Churches could make this obscene river a lovely thing." (Knox could speak perfectly good English, ungnarled by "ach's" and "dinnae's," whenever he felt like it.)

The cat would purr its admiration of his voice, winding itself around his narrow shins. The man would squint about. If they were alone, he would allow the rubbing to continue, melting into it. If someone was watching, Knox would boot the cat out of his way, its tail swishing angrily.

Thank Christ I am off the ship at last. That fat pig-wife of the captain's spying on me everywhere with her pig eyes. The only favour I ever did for her was to tear the dead baby out of her by the feet. Now she wants me. The black sows farrowing on my father's farm sickened me less. And thank Christ to be out of that stinking fo'c's'le. Filth and corruption everywhere. Men opening their breeches to show off the size of their organs. Ship's boys acting as their fancy-women.

But during the storms, the truth flared up in them. Fear bulged in their eyes, and I taunted them all, every single one of them, with the burning fires of hell. I was on deck during the great storm in mid-ocean, admiring the fury of the waters. They were trying to lower sail when a boom snapped, the sail ripped, and sheets flogged everywhere. A young sailor, the worst balls-strutter of the lot, caught his arm in the grip of a ratchet. The bone was half-broken, like a sappy branch, and all the flesh torn, the muscles severed. I took the surgeon's saw and sawed the arm away from his jerking body, then I carried him below and dipped the stump in boiling tar. For days, I was the one to bite off his rotten flesh and suck out the pus. I even swallowed it if they were watching. They couldn't match me. As long as I can remember, death and sickness, sickness and death have been my allies.

Now the voyage is over. This was a good place to land. All around me, beautiful sites for churches, plain churches, with plain cemeteries, no flowers if I can help it. I have planted already the men nobody else would touch, who died of cholera on the voyage. I've manured the soil with corpses the way we did with the dead cattle on the farm. I buried their sad priest, sick since we left France. Only Clootie and I attended his funeral. We commended his body to the devil. Back on the ship, I cleaned the shit and the vomit of the sick from the decks. It gives me an advantage over them all, they are so concerned about staying alive.

The sailors presented the natives with pieces of coloured broken glass, brown wooden beads, pieces of rope, and scraps of cloth. The natives seemed uninterested. One gift only, an iron knife, they all admired. The captain insisted it go to the chief, Quheesquheenay, to win his favour. They offered the natives pieces of Breton cheese, quite rank after the voyage, which the natives, in turn, gave to their dogs; fried chicken legs (chickens had been kept aboard), which the natives relished; boiled chicken eggs, which they spat out. Wine they treated as contaminated water, and could not understand why the sailors drank it when there was so much fresh water around. They munched cautiously on some lumps of black bread from the captain's pantry.

The natives gave little in return, no gold or silver, which was really what the sailors hoped for. They did give them amulets full of rats' giblets and bones. The sailors objected to the smell and threw the amulets into the river while the natives looked on. They invited the crew to eat a sort of stewed beef that smelt very appetizing, but the sailors were afraid it was made of human meat. Some of them vomited spontaneously at the very sight of it. The natives watched all this impassively.

Finally the chief's council offered, as a special treat to the captain, a bowl full of fresh assorted testicles of forest creatures, from the huge rubbery testes of the moose and the bear to the tiny soft beads of rats and rabbits. The captain hid his nausea and diplomatically accepted the gift. He took it back with him aboard ship, and, after dark, flung the testes overboard. They caught in an eddy, and floated around the ship for days, swelling grotesquely till they burst and sank.

The male natives were tall, for the most part, well muscled, dressed in neatly stitched animal skins. Sickness was unusual amongst them. There were no wens, no leprosy, no bloody flux, no stopping of the stomach, no gout, no strangury, no fistulas, no tissicks, no spotted fever, no headmould, no shingles, no rickets, no scurvy, no griping in the guts. There were no congenital deformities. There were no pest-houses.

The skin of the warriors was bronze and clear, except for battle scars. They had flashing dark eyes, and they all seemed to be superb athletes, capable of feats the puny Bretons could only envy. They could lope with ease along tangled forest paths, hurl their spears gracefully, paddle their bark canoes at amazing speeds. They wrestled with ferocity, not hesitating to break an opponent's limb if the opportunity offered.

The natives had heard about the French from neighbouring tribes who had been visited by earlier ships, but this was the first time they themselves had seen the strangers. Clearly they were disappointed, for they found it impossible to respect men whose physical prowess was so defective. But they did respect the power of the arquebuses and the ship's canon, which the Frenchmen quickly demonstrated.

The French sailors learnt to be careful in their approaches to the native women. A warrior's wives were private property and it was death for a stranger to tamper with them. All the other women were available to all the tribe, and were quite free with their sexual favours, even widows and grandmothers. Which was as well for the Frenchmen, since the young women, golden-skinned and lithe, would have nothing to do with them. They had the bodies of dancers. Their clothing was provocative, their breasts dangling loose, their nipples erect when excited, which was often. Their skirts were split to the waist. When they ran, their hairless crotches were visible. Often, while they were relaxing, or were just sitting down, they would finger their groins unconsciously, or sometimes consciously if they saw the Frenchmen squinting at them.

At night the warriors would flit around their bonfires, whooping fearsomely. Or they would stretch on beds of skins moodily sucking on their tobacco pipes with glassy eyes. If the visitors were present, there would be an air of tension. The chief of the tribe, Quheesquheenay, would sit there on his deerskin mat, making no effort to communicate, staring intently at the Frenchmen. The solemn beat of drums would resound, echoed by other drums great distances away across the river.

"Oomhowoomareoomtheoomaliensoom?"

"Oomtheyoomstinkoomouroomvillageoomoutoom."

"Oomkilloomthemoom."

"Oomweoomunlikeoomyouoomonlyoomkilloomworthyoom-
enemiesoom."

"Oomcutoomthemoomupoominoompiecesoom."

"Oomevenoomifoomweoomcutoomthemoomupoominoom-
piecesoomandoomsewedoomalloomtheoombestoompartsoom-
togetheroomweoomstilloomwouldoomnotoomhaveoomaoomreal
oomenemyoomforoomtheiroompenisesoomareoomlikeoom-
wormsoom."

"Oomuseoomtheiroompenisesoomtooomcatchoomfishoom."

"Oomtheoomfishoominoomouroomriveroomareoomtoooom-
smartoomtheyoomknowoomwormsoomareoomnotoomthatoom-
smalloom."

I have the heathen under control. They despise the others but
they fear me. I notice the young braves, showing off to each other
throwing their spears at targets, grow silent even when Clootie
appears amongst them. Their shaman is terrified of the cat.
I am sure he has tried all his curses against me and Clootie in
vain, since the time when the daughter of the chief, Quheesquheenay, developed a terrible fever and was clearly going to die.
The shaman couldn't cure her, he could only make things worse.
The chief was desperate and asked if I could do anything. They
believe that those who are indifferent to death have great power
over life.

What makes John Knox tick? A question he sometimes asks
himself. He tells himself this story:

Once upon a time early in the sixteenth century, a little Scottish
boy lived on a farm near Edinburgh. He was a quick-witted little
boy, too smart by half for his school-fellows, who hated his guts. He
possessed certain time-honoured schoolboy traits: he liked to
pluck the legs and wings from insects to see their reactions. He
possessed, too, certain other traits not so time-honoured: with an
axe, he enjoyed cutting the legs off live rabbits and chickens. From
time to time, he would take pleasure in dropping a dead mouse

into his mother's stew. On such occasions, he would play sick, and reap the double benefit of watching the others eat the stew, and of being himself considered rather delicate. This gained him additional attention. In short, that was the kind of boy he was. A practical joker.

He had many sisters, some of them quite attractive, and no brothers. His attitude towards his sisters was somewhat ambivalent. He hated their guts and would steal their make-up and pinch their arms quite cruelly. But, he liked to peep at them before bedtime, through a crack in his bedroom wall, admiring the breasts and pudenda in their various stages of development. Yes, he found that rather a stimulating part of his day.

His mother and father, it should be noted, were honest-to-goodness farmers, and regular church-goers.

(John Knox always likes the story to this point.)

One of the practical jokes the boy liked to play concerned rats. He would capture rats in a wooden box. Then, when no one was around, he would head on over to the pigsty, and call out the pigs. There was a small round hole through the wall beside the feed-troughs. The boy would chase the rats out of the box, into this hole, and right into the mouths of the pigs. The pigs had grown fond of such a regular treat. This was one prank the boy really enjoyed.

One thing leads to another. It happened that he was looking after his littlest sister, three months old, while his parents were making jams inside the house. As he wandered past the pigsty, carrying the baby, he wondered how the pigs would deal with a tiny pink infant, rather than tiny pink rats. He gently laid the baby on the muddy floor of the sty, and called out the pigs. Well, who knows what goes through a pig's mind? Did they even notice the different proportions, the different texture? Four huge porkers seized the baby limbs, and ripped her to pieces, regardless of her screams, and swallowed her in great slobbering gobbets.

The howls of the baby and the snorting of the pigs attracted the attention of the honest father and mother, and they came running down from the farmhouse to see what was going on. What they saw horrified them. They saw the bloody mess on the sty floor. They saw their little boy looking at them apprehensively.

At that very moment, just then, quite as if by design, the boy found religion. As soon as he saw the genuine anguish on his parents' honest faces, he began to shout, as if by instinct, "O Jesus, O Jesus," and, jumping in amongst the pigs, kicked and slapped at their snouts, shouting, "Begone, Satan, begone," an expression he had often heard from the preachers at the church to which his honest parents took him each Sunday. His father grabbed him by the coat and pulled him out of that sty. The boy said, "I was takin' the babby doon for a walk, when a great hairy black beastie wi' fire comin' oot o' its mooth and its ears pulled the bairnie oot o' ma airms and threw it ower the wa' to the piggies."

He could see that his parents already half-believed him, certain that no human child would be capable of feeding his baby sister to pigs. The boy understood then that all the quirks in himself he had misguidedly thought to be unnatural and perverse were really, if properly perceived, signs of a religious disposition. And so he decided that, as soon as he grew up, he would become a Reformer. And he did. His parents became, in due course, very proud of his achievements, though he sometimes thought he could see a scep-tical glint in their eyes. But they all lived happily ever after.

Such is the tale John Knox tells himself: he knows it doesn't cover all the bases, but it is generally quite pleasing. One thing still sur-prises him after all these years: when alone, religious matters never enter his head. He wonders if the other Reformers are the same, but hesitates to ask.

With my pussy-cat, Clootie, I went to her tepee. As we entered, a sweaty young man left, hitching up his loincloth. The tepee was all shadows and foul smells, the shaman's smoke. The girl lay on a frame bed of stretched skins, staring at the roof. She was naked, and she too was covered in sweat. Her legs were parted and her hand was at her crotch, fingers stroking. The chief, two of his coun-cillors, and the shaman, stood beside the bed. He is a mouth-shaman, and was leaning over her spitting some green mixture into her mouth. I saw her spit most of it right back in his face, and vomit up the rest. The shaman looked fierce with his red and white stripes, but his eyes were anxious. He shook his rattles and howled, but they all knew, and he knew, he had failed. The girl looked over at me and smiled, the shreds of vomit around her mouth. She lifted her hand from her crotch, and stretched it out to me, her fingers glistening.

She had sweated out her disease, her *furor uterinus* for days, and she would die soon, for they did not know how to save her. All they could think of was to supply her with men to satisfy her deadly appetite and to trust in the shaman's superstitious mumbo-jumbo.

"That hill, over there by the sacrificial stakes, would be a good spot for a church."

"Ah, yes."

"The long-house would be all right as a temporary church, but they'd have to strip away those ornamental scalps and skulls."

"Indeed."

"If we burnt down the whole forest on the peninsula and ripped up the weeds and the flowers, and anything else alive, we could build a whole set of churches, one for every day of the week. Nothing fancy, no ornaments or any of that kind of thing, just plain seats and a stool for the preacher. Cats would be welcome. We'd have plain cemeteries with picket fences for each church.

"Interesting."

"How about a church under that waterfall? Made of fieldstone, very plain. You'd have to carry an umbrella for going in and out. A nice effect."

"Quite so."

I told them I must have absolute freedom in the treatment of the girl or I would do nothing. I ordered the shaman out with his barbarous cures. He mumbled at me, cursing me, no doubt, in his heathen way. I wouldn't let him away with that, but I replied moderately, damning him only according to the Scriptures. Clootie, as ever, snarling at him with hunched back, terrified him, and he hurried out of the tepee, along with the chief and the others. I called in two of the older sailors to help me begin this holy work.

First we forced her hands away from her groin. We lashed her hands and her feet to the sides of the crib to stop her thrashing about. She sweated even more and began screaming. I opened my Bible in my left hand and, from under my coat, I unsheathed my whip, which I had brought with me on purpose.

Everything was ready. I ordered the sailors to stand outside the entrance of the tepee, and allow no one to enter. I began to read from the Book of Psalms in a loud voice, uncoiling my whip slowly before the patient's eyes. Clootie jumped onto the bed and rubbed himself against her.

My wounds stink and are corrupt because of my foolishness.
For my loins are filled with a loathsome disease: and there is
no soundness in my flesh.
Thou shalt break them with a rod of iron.
The heathen are sunk down in the pit that they made.
Upon the wicked thou shalt rain snares, fire and brimstone,
and an horrible tempest: this shall be the portion of their cup.
Then did I beat them small as the dust before the wind.
And I smote his enemies in the lower parts:
I put them to a perpetual reproach.

I began to read the verses a second time, more loudly. But this time, after each verse, I lashed her naked body. She screamed as the skin lifted, the welts rose across her breasts. Then I aimed lower on her body, across the thighs and the open vulva. She stopped screaming. She gave great gasps and whimpers, and it was my turn to roar. I shouted the verses and lashed harder and harder. Her body convulsed, and, at last, the demon rushed out between her legs in a liquid gurgle. Clootie, who had been rubbing himself against her all through this, howled, and his hair stood on end. I myself was roused by that evil in her. To ensure it was completely gone, I lashed her several more times. Then I put my hand cautiously towards her groin, fearful of the bite of the beast. With my fingers I could feel nothing at the entrance, so I slid them into the round, moist cavern. Still nothing to be afraid of. Unsatisfied, I inserted the long sweaty handle of my whip, turning it, moving it in and out, in and out, the sure way to scrape any remnants of the demon away. Her eyes glazed as she looked up at me, thankful for my precautions. I jerked the handle up and down rapidly, she convulsed again, sighed, and immediately fell asleep. I too was drained by my exorcism, but satisfied. I knew that all was well.

I sat for a moment to catch my breath, then I opened the tepee flap and let the chief and his men back in. I sensed their revulsion as they saw on her body the stripes of the lash. Yet she was in a deep, untroubled sleep and her fever was broken. I expected no thanks and received none. The shaman untied the ropes, and covered her sleeping body with skins. I told the chief that somebody must administer the same cure to her each time she fell into that fever. I told him, though I am not sure he understood, that he must build churches, churches, churches, in memory of her cure.

"You tell us we should not eat our enemies, yet the captain says that in France, he and his men eat Jehovah daily. Explain this."

"Filthy heathen, spare me your quibbles."

"Before original sin, did men still fart and shit after they ate?"

"Filthy heathen, you do not understand."

"What good is heaven if all our tribe do not go to heaven? What good is heaven if my wives and my sons and my dogs are not in heaven with me? What good is heaven if my enemies are not there so that we can all reminisce together in heaven about old battles?"

"Filthy heathen, cease your blasphemy."

"How can you hate the women and yet desire them so much at the same time?"

"Filthy, lying heathen. You are one of the damned."

How ugly the aliens are, their skin is wormy white and marred by scabs. Boils sprout on them overnight like forest toadstools. Their clothing is clumsy and heavy. Their minds are a mystery. They adore their Book, a collection of dead words. We would have annihilated them long ago, but for their guns. We have never before faced enemies who were contemptible as men, yet could defeat us in battle because of their weapons.

Their shaman, the little man, Knox, is the living death. He has made a few converts amongst our people, even my own daughter. Pain was his gift to her. The captain, a simple man, admits that many like Knox will come to our hunting grounds in the future. Our own shaman has dreamed, for three nights, the end of the world.

"I am curious about the function of your shamans across the ocean. Here, our shaman prays for good luck, curses bad luck, sings songs and tells good stories at our feasts, blesses the penis and vagina of the newly-weds, teaches the children how to bind arrows well, how to be brave in battle. He defies the demons of darkness; in times of famine, he fasts and moves his tepee to the forest so that the rest of us may eat well and live in company in the village. He weeps for all the dead, he rejoices at births. He loves the river, the trout, the moose, the eagle, the pack-wolves, the musk-rats, the morning sun, the snow in winter. He is the friend of our friends, he admires the ferocity of our enemies. Nothing that exists disgusts him."

"He is a filthy heathen fiend and is already damned."

Their stay amongst us has lasted only two moons. They must sail away before the winter storms. They have wiped out all game within six miles of the village — we will now face a hard winter. Some of our children have died of a cough we have never known. As a final gesture, the aliens say they will kill for us, with their guns, our enemies in a neighbouring village. I have thanked them and refused their offer. Our shaman is glad they are leaving, but he still whispers to me that he sees only death in his omens.

One night around midnight, while the village fires were still flickering, two huge marauding bears came barging out of the forest. Knox's cat, Clootie, fur on end, charged at them screeching from deep in his throat. The bears, startled, turned and ran. For days afterwards, Knox would wheeze with laughter at the memory. "Ach, Clootie," he would say, "ane wee Scottish cratur is mair than a match for a' the beasties in the New Warld."

Some thoughts on a brief code of behaviour to be followed by converts after I am gone
A. *Sexual Matters* Strict monogamy is a must, even bestiality is a lesser offence than adultery; sexual intercourse only for breeding; cover the flesh: shirts and trousers for men, underwear and breast-bindings for women; absolutely no kissing, cuddling, or touching

of the body of the other sex before marriage; the menstrual abomination to be dealt with in complete secrecy by the women.
B. *Other* Hunting needs to be organized on a less seasonal basis to keep the men from being idle for lengthy spells; rites of passage for the boys should not be discouraged, the pain being a valuable discipline; likewise the practice of torturing enemies: it teaches contempt of the flesh (much of these heathens' behaviour may be turned to good account).
C. *Build churches, churches.*

The French captain (his wife was party to it) coaxed one of the older native women to be his mistress. She would then gossip with the other women about his fat paunch and his stinking breath. And about how, with his wife looking on, he always made love to her from behind like a dog. Whenever the captain appeared in the village afterwards, Knox would trot in front of him, barking as loudly as he could. All the village dogs would join the chorus. Some of the native women, inspired by this, would squat on the ground and urinate, as the captain passed, their tongues dangling like those of hounds.

We will root out the shaman Knox's followers after he has gone. Even my own daughter. We will saw off their heads with the iron knife they gave me, then we will throw the bodies and the knife into the river. Nothing of him will remain. He longs to return to his homeland where his enemies are more like him. We are too inno-cent for his liking. This alone is certain: we are our only friends.

The day before they were due to sail, a native guide led a group of sailors through the forest and showed them a mound of earth in a clearing. Knox and his cat Clootie went with them, as always, when there was the prospect of some hunting. The sailors began digging in the mound, hoping to find some of that elusive treasure. Instead, skulls. Hundreds upon hundreds of human skulls. They presumed they were in some kind of traditional tribal burial place. But the skulls, belonging to men, women and children, all seemed recent. Perhaps some disease was responsible. Then they noted that many of the skulls had been split, pierced with sharp objects. They saw too, that the bone had not been picked clean by worms and ants. The guide told them the mound was the top of a shaft, hundreds of feet deep, and that it was the place where they had, for generations, buried the heads of enemies who had been decapitated. Their heads were boiled, he said, their brains eaten. In the last three moons before the sailors arrived, he said, Quheesquheenay's people had beheaded in this way at least one thousand enemies, and had filled the pit to overflowing. On the basis of that good omen, the arrival of the aliens had been welcomed. Some of the men were appalled, but Knox laughed heartily. They lacked faith, he said: it was clear from the Bible that Providence frequently operated by means of a timely massacre or two. Knox secretly suspected that Quheesqueenay had arranged the "discovery" to deter the Frenchmen from ever returning to the New World.

The coastline of France looms in the distance. Knox alone, of those on deck, does not need to be there. He relishes the ferocious cold, the thin snow falling in a gusty wind. The coastal hills are dappled with it, like leprosy. Or is it, he smiles, heaven's vomit? Clootie would have purred at the idea. Clootie who is not with him. Clootie who had to be left behind, prowling, he imagines, those forest thickets, terrifying man and beast for years yet, especially that old heathen shaman. Reminding them of something they would not easily destroy. He thinks of Clootie with fondness but with no regret. The New World was child's play. Now the battle will be amongst professionals, like himself. He breathes deeply, fills his lungs with the chill air sweeping over the water from all the chill regions of the Old World. His home.

Edward and Georgina

Edward and Georgina

There is no shortage of rumours about the Byfields. The Byfields, Edward and Georgina, brother and sister. Edward the meek, Georgina the strong. They live among the down-and-outs and the still-hopefuls in a building of clapboard that buckles from age and neglect. Edward has a steady job, but lacks ambition. He is content to remain here, in his shabby apartment in this octoplex spawned by an opulent mansion from a dead age.

If he is a middle-sized, middle-aged man (he is about fifty), she is of imposing height for a woman of similar age. He is heavy and pale. She is thick-set but always ruddy-faced. Though the colour must be the product of make-up, for she doesn't go out much. When she does emerge, her neighbours hear the spiking of her semi-high heels on the brown linoleum of the stairway, less hollow in the hall, resonant again on the sidewalk. She walks upright, her black wig leaking wisps of grey.

The neighbours believe that, silent though she is, she is in charge. They say Georgina and Edward are a combination of opposites. The empress and her eunuch.

Rumours cling to them. Unrefined rumours, because no one really cares much about them. For the Byfields are remote, grotesque as circus clowns. Of their past, all anyone knows for sure is that they came from England years ago. For the present, it is enough that they share, with all the tenants of the octoplex, a communal smell of ragouts, pastas, goulashes, curries and fricassees that mingle without much acrimony in the hallways. Is there in it too a tinge of mothballs? Or of decay?

Edward shows no interest in women. At his job with the Parks Department (in summer he operates a lawn-mower, in winter a mini snow-plough) the young men tease him:

"You're not past it yet, Ed. You come with us tonight and we'll fix you up."

Edward invariably refuses, unsmiling. He may say, in his flat North-of-England accent:

"Georgina wouldn't like that at all."

They are certain that he is touched, and queer. Occasionally, stifling laughter, they'll plead with him for a date with Georgina. Edward is always indignant and suggests they've no chance with her. He never tells them why. They suspect he is jealous.

The lives of Edward and Georgina seem to dovetail perfectly. Neighbours note that on weekday mornings and afternoons the TV blares in their apartment. Georgina accepts no callers. Newspaper boys and Jehovah's Witnesses have long ago recognized the futility of trying to get her attention during the daytime.

Then at five o'clock, Edward returns from work. Promptly Georgina emerges, freshly made-up, revitalized. She descends upon the corner store to garner odds and ends for dinner. Or visits the laundromat where she ostentatiously washes Edward's soiled uniform. Meantime, no doubt, he relaxes at home, weary after another day of toil with the Parks Department.

On summer weekends, other families, to escape the city, endure the windblown confinement of overloaded cars and head for the lake. Edward and Georgina, car-less, prefer to stay at home. Georgina, who rarely speaks, is reported to have said to a neighbour in her sonorous voice:

"It's so quiet when everyone goes away in the summer. Just right for Edward."

But every two years, nevertheless, they do spend a week at the lake together. Edward talks about it in advance at work, vague as to destination, but firm as to purpose:

"It'll be good for Georgina, you know."

Implying that he himself would rather not. He asks a neighbour to keep an eye on the apartment while they're away. He does not hand over the key, however, for he says he dislikes the thought of anyone prying around amongst Georgina's intimate possessions. The neighbours are used to his candour.

Then they're gone. No one sees them leave, early in the morning, though one or two people could swear they heard them go. From their apartment, no rasping of floorboards, no clanking of dishes, no insistent TV laughter, no gargling of pipes, no penetrating whispers. During the next week, now Edward, furtive and unnatural, now Georgina, self-possessed, may be glimpsed at far Wasaga Beach, or maybe Port Elgin, amongst the genuine holiday-makers. They will send a card to their neighbour: "Having a lovely time. Home soon." It will be variously signed, "Edward and Georgina," "Georgina and Edward," or, "The Byfields." The hand is unmistakable, lurching to the left or to the right in an erratic scrawl.

Seven days pass and they're home again. Early in the morning, the sounds of their presence permeate the apartment. Neighbours look out for them. Georgina appears at the corner store, glad to be back. Their absence was a hastily corrected wobble in the constant orbit of their lives.

Rumours. That they are not really brother and sister, but lovers, fugitives from some long-forgotten romantic disgrace. (No one wishes to envy them, so that rumour dies.) That they are indeed brother and sister, living incestuously. That they fled from England to be free to pursue their illicit love. (Some of the women are convinced that Georgina has too knowing a look, and wonder how she got it.) That he is an IRA informer, living incognito; a convicted strangler out on probation. That she is a countess who married beneath herself; a defrocked nun; a prostitute who knows Edward's guilty secret.

Life may end, rumour lives on. In an unusually cool September, Edward falls sick. He takes a few days off work, feels no better, and goes at last to see a doctor. The diagnosis is not good. Edward ought to slow down or there will be dire consequences.

He returns to his job and tells his co-workers that he must be careful:

"I've to stop burning the candle at both ends."

They do not laugh for they see in his eyes that he is unwell. He is worried about Georgina, and they urge him to be careful for her sake:

"She'd be lost without you."

He agrees with them.

The neighbours note that Georgina herself seems out of sorts, worried over Edward. She is careless about her make-up, even more careless about her clothes. Sickness brings out the family resemblance between the two. To inquiries about Edward's health, she shakes her head miserably and will say nothing.

On a cold morning in December, Edward collapses near his snow-plough. In the freshly fallen snow, his body duplicates itself in intaglio, with angel wings. A passer-by finds him, a taxi rushes him to Emergency. He is grey, grim. The nurse asks him about next of kin and he gives Georgina's name; he mutters:

"Don't send for her, leave her alone, I'm all right."

But he isn't all right. Before his own doctor arrives, Edward is dead.

Georgina can't be reached. It is impossible to phone, for Edward refused to have a phone in their apartment; it caused too much unwanted disturbance. A police sergeant is sent to break the bad news to her and find out what she wants done with her brother's body. No one answers his knock though he can hear the sound of the TV quite clearly through the door. The neighbours say they haven't seen much of Georgina lately at the store or the laundromat. That decides the sergeant. With the help of a fellow-officer, he forces the door of the apartment.

The smell seems stronger inside. The entranceway is tidy enough, some coats draped over wall hooks. Then a living-room with a brown rug, stuffed couch, and chair: a still life with black-

and-white TV. One of the policemen switches it off. Silence. Faint noises from the street penetrate the window in the niche of the kitchen. The open bedroom door reveals a disordered double bed, a brown varnished dresser with an android plaster head, on which sits Georgina's black wig. The last door, shut, leads to the bathroom. The smell in the apartment is oppressive as the sergeant slowly turns the knob.

The door swings back, clangs heavily against the rim of a chipped enamel bath tub. "Empty," "No one Here," it gongs. The policemen are relieved. They can do no more. They leave a note for Georgina and ask the neighbours to watch out for her return.

Three days pass. Still no sign of Georgina. Edward's funeral takes place, only a single representative of the Parks Department in attendance, bringing a wreath of imported narcissus. The clergyman on duty did not know Edward. He murmurs appropriate prayers as the coffin discreetly slides through the curtain to test the efficiency of the Cremato-Gas Furnace.

Where is Georgina? She is needed to accept the offerings of the insurance company, to receive the other official relics of Edward's life. For the sake of tidiness, Georgina must be found. Georgina must be found.

But there never was a Georgina. There never was a Georgina to find. The insurance detective sensed that immediately. A reliable man, near retirement age, he loved his daughters and his grandchildren above everything. He understood at once why so few of Georgina's things remained. The shabby black coat, yes; the old fashioned high-heeled shoes, the florid dress, the patched blue underclothes in need of cleaning. But where were the purse, the photographs? What about the jewel-box, the fading letters, the Harlequin romances, the tokens of a past that should have cluttered the case? His instincts, alert to every kind of seedy deception, led him straight to the truth. Georgina did not exist.

No, she did not exist. Edward had never had a sister. Was it the wig on its androgynous skull that gave the game away? The detective was not fooled by the female paraphernalia, the plastic bag full of lipsticks and rouges left lying in the bathroom that led the police (so mechanical in these matters) to deduce that Georgina had packed her suitcase and left town in a hurry.

He introduced himself to the neighbours and coaxed them (he had an air of dependability — it was, with his white hair, his strong point) to tell him about the Byfields. Everything they said made him more certain. Always, in all seasons, Georgina had worn the shiny black coat, the florid dress protruding obscenely, the black shoes clumping. They had often seen the fringe of phoney black hair (a plain woman's conceit, they thought) under a multi-coloured headscarf with scenes from Niagara Falls. He had found the scarf, still tucked inside her coat sleeve. Sometimes she seemed to them like a witch in all that make-up, unseemly in an elderly woman.

But none of them remembered, no, not once, ever seeing Georgina and Edward together over the years.

During a last, reluctant search of the apartment — the smell offended him — the detective found, as he knew he would, the final evidence: a letter, recently written. It lay under the brown-paper lining of the dresser's bottom drawer. He recognized the crude handwriting he had seen on the holiday post-cards:

Dearest Georgina, my ever-loving sister,
                    I hope this finds you well. My old "ticker" (ha! ha!) is not so good now as you already know, but you're not to worry about what will happen to you when your Edward is gone away. What I want to say is "Chin up!!" I'm sure you'll be "hunky dory" without me to worry about. Just keep "a stiff upper lip!!" as they used to say, and remember me and then I won't really be gone at all!! We've had some lovely cries together, haven't we, dearest Georgina? But I hope this letter isn't making you cry. Before I had you, my lovely sister, I didn't want to live any more! Can you believe that?? I must have been going "off my rocker!!" as they say. But then I had the loving friendship of a dear, sweet, lovely sister (this is very "luvvy-duvvy!!"). I had someone to "have a chat with" at last. Now when I feel so ill I know you're always with me. No real brother and sister could have been happier than us, and I know our lovely lovely "secret" (three guesses!!) will last forever and for-

ever. Never never forget me and rest assured I am,

Your "best friend,"

Sincerely,

Edward Byfield.

XXXXXXX Love and Kisses!!

The detective folded the letter carefully and put it in his briefcase. He closed the apartment door quietly behind him as though not to disturb sleepers.

He was not a callous man. His daughters' happy marriages, his affection for his grandchildren filled his life. He felt only pity for Edward Byfield and all the other subterranean lives his work obliged him to wrestle out into the light. This investigation was almost complete: it would do no harm, it would be a kindness to Edward's memory to leave the neighbours to their illusions. For them, Georgina had existed even more concretely than her anaemic creator. Even if Edward had invented Georgina for some other, fraudulent end, his own death had, ironically, thwarted it. So he would report the whole truth only to headquarters, and assure his employers that the case could be discreetly closed.

But now rumours have begun again. The detective hears reports daily of her movements: Georgina disappearing into a crowd of shoppers in Market Square; Georgina's unmistakable back receding along King Street on a busy Saturday morning; the sound of Georgina's shoes ricocheting at night down the alley towards the corner store; Georgina glimpsed on a passing bus, her wig askew, her make-up vivid as always.

There is a rumour that Georgina, less reticent than before, has told some neighbourhood children she'll be back one of these days to collect Edward's things. These rumours are hard to pin down, and the detective is disturbed by them. One particular rumour fills him with dread. It is said that Georgina has been spotted walking in the park, accompanied by Edward, pale and heavy as ever. This is the first time Edward and Georgina have ever been seen together. The detective has asked to be taken off the case. He spends all his spare time with his daughters and his grandchildren and waits with growing impatience for his retirement.

Captain Joe

Captain Joe

That's Captain Joe on the right. There he stands, caught in the sepia print on page two of this album, its pages in tatters, reliquary of a family heritage. Notice how in these old pictures they'd look straight at the camera and smile. Except for Captain Joe. The Grandfather smiles there beside him. Does anyone, aside from me, remember these men from another time, a distant world? See how they're dressed: trousers bag, boots curl. But the Grandfather wears a shirt with long sleeves, no collar. The Captain, it seems, prefers wool, the black sweater of a fisherman. He wears a sailor's skipped cap, his left hand grips something — a pipe, maybe. He looks just like a captain. But he does not smile, he looks intently at the mechanical eye as it transfixes him in time.

In 1940 he arrived in that village in Central Scotland. Because of the sailor's cap, they called him Captain. A man of about sixty, he looked his age. But he had never been a sailor though he had lived near the sea. The villagers thought him a curiosity — a Perth man, at least a hundred miles from home, who wanted to live with them. It was a village of Irish immigrants who worked in the only industry, the iron foundry. And it was wartime, but their job exempted them from conscription into the army.

The Captain found things to do around the village. He sickled the grass that choked the cinder paths and he cleaned the soot from out-of-the-way windows. At length he became the village's alarm clock. In the mornings at six he would knock on the doors of the day-shift workers, shocking them out of dreams or embraces into the bitterness of the dawn. So he made enough to pay the rent of a small row house, buy his food and tobacco. The older men took to him, yet wondered why this quiet Scotsman had chosen their village.

The Grandfather hit it off with the Captain from the first, and the boy liked to be with them. Those were the only times the Captain laughed: the boy felt his laugh hadn't grown as old as the rest of him because it hadn't had much use. They would play draughts together. The boy enjoyed a game with Captain Joe, for he didn't play with the guile of the Grandfather or any of the other men, so the boy could beat him. After school he often went over to the Captain's little house for a cup of tea. They'd play draughts till his brother's shout of "Dinner's ready!" signalled last moves.

Nothing lasts forever. During the Captain's second winter in the village he began to die. He would sometimes be so sick, creases in his face, that draughts would cease for weeks on end. The Grandfather used to sit by his bed most of the time: two quiet men, they might exchange an odd word, or the Grandfather might read him pieces from the newspaper, or they might doze like two old friends.

A district nurse called in to see the Captain daily. She and the Grandfather between them made sure he ate something, that he was not too uncomfortable, for he did not complain. The boy visited him some evenings so that the Grandfather could go to his daughter's for a decent meal. Captain Joe's bed had been removed from the cell of a bedroom into the living-room. A coal-fire's glow fended off the night chills.

One evening when the boy came in, the Captain looked much better (that was the way the sickness now affected him). He was up out of bed, his sailor's cap on, looking as though he was waiting just for the boy. The cup of tea was ready, but he did not want to play draughts.

"No draughts tonight. I want to say some things while I'm in the mood."

The boy was taken aback: he wasn't used to having grown-ups confide in him. He'd rather have played draughts. On went the Captain:

"A while back, I told the Grandfather about my life before I came here. I was going to tell you too, but I didn't want to frighten you. The Grandfather thinks there's no harm in it now. I know what they say about me: Isn't it queer for a man my age to come and settle here? — Surely there's something wrong with a man who leaves his family and friends in wartime when nobody knows what'll happen next? They're right. I came from Perth, up in the Highlands where it's clean and fresh, not like down here. I was a grocer there. In the mornings when I arrived at the shop, I used to cut myself a slice of hot bread, plaster the yellow butter on it, and wash it down with a glass of cold milk. I can still taste it. I think that was what I liked most about a grocer's job."

The Captain breathed deeply. Then he told how, when he was eighteen, he met a girl called Laura. They went out together for a year, then, like everybody else in those days, they got married. That was in 1900. He was young and healthy — on Sundays he used to climb for miles up into the hills to catch the big brown spotted trout for dinner. Laura liked to fry them. He said he used to call her his "Fair Maid of Perth… ."

The memories hurt. Captain Joe's eyes spouted tears. The boy was full of embarrassment for him. He had never seen a man cry. He watched the bowed head of the Captain, the fingers that made a cage over his face, tips buried in his grey hair.

The Captain wiped his eyes with a rag, made no excuses:

"One night that November I worked late and walked home after dark. There was a chill in the air, there were no stars out and nobody in the streets. When I got home, I felt tired but good. I ate some supper and sat for a bit by the fire. I went to bed around mid-night, cuddled in against Laura in the cold sheets, and slept."

What a sleep it was.

"I never slept like that before. When I woke my head was full of a dream about an old man. I couldn't remember his face, but the dream was about all the things he'd done in his life. I was glad the dream was over, for I felt like a peeping Tom.

"But the memory wouldn't go away. I turned to Laura for comfort. My God! The face beside me was the face of a grey-haired old
woman. I pulled back from her. I must still be asleep, for my bones
were all aching like an old man's, and there was an awful taste in my
mouth. The skin on the back of my hand was wrinkled like an old
man's skin. This was a nightmare, and I just wanted to be out of it.
There was something about that man in the dream that upset me.
It was like recognizing parts of a book I knew I'd read a long time
ago. Then I remembered the man's face clearly, just for a split
second. It was an old man's face, but it was in some ways very like my
own. I began to sweat. I slid out of the bed and shuffled across the
linoleum to a mirror on a dark wardrobe by the fireplace. A face
stared back at me. It was the face in the dream, and it was my own
face, the way it would look when I was old. It was my own reflection
I saw in that mirror."

The Captain and the boy were silent. The Captain looked like a
sick man again, his face like chalk, so that the boy was worried
about him and rose to go for help.

"It's all right. Just wait a minute. Hand me that glass of water."

The boy was afraid, not only because the Captain looked so ill,
but because the story scared him. But he wanted to hear it out and
the Captain wanted to finish.

"I went to sleep on a November night in 1900. When I woke and
looked in that wardrobe mirror, it was a morning of November in
1940, and I was sixty years old. I mean what I'm saying. I was a boy
when I went to bed, an old man when I woke. If I did wake. At the
time they thought I was mad and confined me to bed because I
kept saying it was all a bad dream. It would have been better to say
nothing. How could I ever prove to them that it was a mistake? I
even knew their names and faces — I'd seen them in the dream.
They laughed at me for saying I was only a twenty-year-old boy.
They seemed so sure of themselves I sometimes caved in. I felt I'd
been cheated out of a life. Then I would cry in front of that old
woman, Laura. She didn't like that — a man of sixty should have
more self-control. But she had had years to learn to be old, and I
was a newcomer to it."

One morning, the Captain said, when he was by himself in the house, he opened the wardrobe and found clothes and a seaman's cap. He was surprised they fitted so well. He went to the desk where the old woman kept her purse. He took a few pound notes and slipped out the side door. He never went back.

He'd been on the move ever since. He lived for a week here, a week there, Aberdeen, Stirling, Glasgow. When he would feel bad, he'd try to tell someone what had happened to him. It was a sure way to lose friends. He had learnt one thing: there was no help for a man like him. It was better to suffer in silence.

"After I left Glasgow, I came here. I liked it that the people were all immigrants. They're all lost too. It's a good place to wait and see how things work out. The Grandfather knew there was something wrong right away: he coaxed it out of me. I think he believes me. Maybe you'll believe me too. One thing. There's no reason for me to be afraid of death. Everybody knows you can't die in a dream, you can only wake up. I love to go to sleep at night. I always hope that in the morning I'll open my eyes and I'll be back in Perth, only it'll be forty years ago, the sun at the bedroom window, Laura there, and our whole lives ahead. We'll laugh about this weird dream. If those forty years can disappear so easily, surely they can come back the same way?"

Captain Joe looked tired, but he had told his story. He thought he'd go to bed now. So the boy went out into the night air and hurried the few yards home.

The Grandfather was waiting for him at the door. He had his cap on, a scarf around his mouth to protect him from the cold, so that only his eyes were visible. He asked how the Captain was, for he was going over to sit with him for a while. He looked at the boy, and the boy had to ask:

"Do you think what he says could have happened?"

"Do you think the Captain's a liar?"

"No, no! but what an awful thing. How could someone young have a dream and wake up an old man?"

The boy could no longer see the Grandfather's eyes.

"That would be very sad, you're right."

And then:

"Would it be less sad if an old man had a dream, and woke up believing he was really only a young man, even though everybody thought he was mad?"

That was what he said. Then he put his hand on the boy's shoulder as he always did to bid him goodnight, and went off into the dark.

Well, of course, I was that boy. I was that boy and I made up my mind, right then, to find out the truth. I would ask the Captain next time I saw him all about his life in Perth, about Laura and that old woman, about his travels before he reached the village. I would ask him (for this troubled me) how, if it was all a dream, the Grand-father and I fitted in.

I did not get a chance to ask my questions. Three days later, Captain Joe died in his sleep with the Grandfather beside his bed. They sent news of his death to Perth, but no word ever came back. The village arranged a funeral for him. The Grandfather took me into the little house where some people were gathered for a last look at the Captain in his coffin (they didn't use to mind exposing children to the dead). Over the body of his friend he whispered to me:

"I wonder if he's finally awake?"

I had no answer for him. I looked down at the face of Captain Joe. On it there was, as usual, no smile. Yet it had about it something strangely youthful in its final, absolute repose.

The Swath

The Swath

This is its first anniversary. It began (I am one of those not afraid to remember it) on this very day a year ago, as dawn was breaking over the prairies. Though it disturbed at first only the monotonous chorales of crickets and bullfrogs, seismographs all over the world immediately started to scrawl out their alerts. Richter Scales registered an unwavering "8". The phenomenon lasted for precisely twenty-four hours, then, with precision, stopped. Those are the facts. Whether the acknowledgement of them will help prepare us for a recurrence is questionable, though, for all I know, elaborate systems of alarms are by now in place. Nor can I say with any assurance what lesson we are supposed to have learnt.

The time, as I said, was dawn, 6 A.M. on the morning of Sunday, July 7th, near the town of Trempe, Saskatchewan, Canada, 52 degrees latitude, 108 degrees longitude. Such details are important. As the sun started to colour the eastern sky, a fissure began to open on the misty surface of the prairie. A fissure with a remarkable property. It streaked towards the west, moving at a constant speed of one thousand miles an hour, leaving in its wake a chasm three hundred feet in width, one hundred feet in depth, with walls and bottom smooth as marble. As though, while the first rays of sunlight mingled with the dawn mist, the first strip of an endless pink lawn was being mowed, the first swath of the earth itself.

The human being who first observed the swath lived not far from Trempe. The swath lipped his clapboard prairie farmhouse. George Ferguson was his name, a sensible man, forty years a rancher. It was his usual time for waking. In his half-sleep he heard a pleasant swishing sound, like a prairie morning wind. He did not hear, because it made no sound, the annihilation of part of his house: the part with the bedroom in which his son, George Jr, nine-teen, slept, the part with the bedroom in which his son, Peter, seventeen, slept, and the part with the kitchen in which his wife, Martha, following her early morning custom of many years, sat sharing honeyed toast with Robbie, the black farm-dog, before making George's breakfast. So it was that in an instant, whilst George Jr was snoring loudly, Peter was dreaming one of his strange erotic dreams, Martha was patting Robbie's black head, Robbie was licking his black lips with his long pink tongue, they all vanished.

A surprise, then, awaits George Ferguson this prairie summer morning. He awakes as usual, yawns, slithers out of bed and shuf-fles towards the bathroom door. He fumbles it ajar. Sees everything. This practical man is the first man to open his eyes on the miracle. His bathroom, once bounded by walls and window, equipped with bath, hand-basin, toilet, adorned with shaving mirror, comb, brush, glass for dentures, and wall cabinet, is transformed. The outside half of the room has been removed with absolute neatness and precision, like the hinged section of a bizarre doll's house. The win-dow, for example, is cut down the middle, as are the bath, the hand-basin and the mirror. Only half of the tumbler in which his den-tures have soaked nightly for twenty years remains. With passing interest (he may still be dreaming) he notes that half of the water that was once in the glass and half of the dentures are still there — as though in a trick glass. Through the gaping wall, he can see the vast expanse of the swath itself, and on the far precipice, through the morning mist, he can make out faintly the shapes of his herd of black and white Holsteins, he can hear their distant lowing as they crane perplexedly towards the house.

After a quick survey of the rest of the house, George Ferguson acknowledges everything: the swath, the evaporation of the two bedrooms, two boys, kitchen, wife and dog. But, ever a practical man, he has to chuckle at the neatness of the swath. There are no frayed ends of pipes, wires, walls. The steep sides of the swath itself are smooth, no untidy roots or rocks protruding, the geological strata well defined as in a sandwich. The swath is as clean as any groove made by router or chisel, clean as any joint which must accommodate some other piece. There is no debris alongside the swath, no rubble on top, no edgeworks. Everything is as clean, George Ferguson tells himself, as a whistle.

He begins to laugh. He laughs, and he laughs, surprising himself. He laughs at the fate of his two loyal sons, he laughs at the disappearance of his good old wife, and he laughs at the loss of his affectionate dog. Still laughing, this practical man turns his attention to the problem of reaching the cattle moaning to him across that great abyss.

The swath, all this while, swept on west, neatly cleaving the highway in front of twenty-three pick-up trucks and seventy-nine private cars leaving (according to the box-office clerk) the all-night quadruple-feature at the *Rodeo* drive-in movie theatre. The occupants of the vehicles, their minds still conditioned to accept the marvellous, strolled to the edge of the abyss, and stared in good-humoured amazement into the gulf left by the swath. There is a report that, nearby, a house was on fire. Its owner, an elderly lady, the relative of an English duchess, sat on the manicured lawn in front of the house playing her accordion. The swath swept away house, lady, and lawn minutes before the Fire Department could reach the scene.

The swath's progress was a wonder to see. Gently it peeled away a strip of the foothills of the Rockies. It made an incision through Jasper National Park. Mount Robson received that neck shave that was so fetching to all who saw it. Campers tell of a beautiful young woman, quite naked, in the woods around the mountain at that time. In the dawn mist she stood breast-feeding a handsome Clydesdale horse. The swath took them to itself.

The swath now approaches the Fraser River. For the first time, its remarkable effect on rivers, lakes and oceans becomes evident. The swath charges right into the Fraser, excising a path through the river bed and out the other side. Even though there is now a three-hundred-foot gap in it, the river seems to flow on as usual. The water reaches the point where the swath bisects it, disappears completely for three hundred feet, then reappears, flowing just as strongly. The two ends of the interrupted river are smooth as walls of glass, the river itself visible in cross-section through them. As though in some trick with mirrors. Salmon, trout and all the other fish discover, however, that there is no water in the gap — they fall out of the two walls of water into the damp furrow. This phenomenon is not to be explained lightly.

The swath then began descending the seaboard side of the Rockies in a more southerly direction, thrusting eagerly towards the Pacific. Moving at the same speed as the earth itself, it plunged into the cool waters of the Hecate Strait and struck the Queen Charlotte Islands, grooving them as neatly as with a chain-saw. Zoologists regret to report that the rarely seen eight-legged moose was grazing in its path. It has not been sighted since. Nor have the remnants of the once-glorious Shabana tribe of Coastal Indians, whose village was in the way. They, at least, were used to the idea of annihilation, and for years their shamans had predicted the imminence of the final swish of the Raven's wings. In the dawn light, the swath rushed at last into the open sea.

   In July, the North Pacific bustles with business and pleasure, pleasure and business, fishing vessels and cruise boats, freighters and sailboats. The swath's journey could not pass unobserved. The coal-freighter, the *S.S. Hamilton*, reported it. Her radar operator picked up something impossible, an undeviating line not far ahead, moving at one thousand miles an hour across the water, leaving a permanent trace on his screen. The ship at once hove to.

   As the dawn light strengthened, the ship steamed cautiously ahead. The watch, from high on the mast, reported to the deck that, dead ahead, the water was furrowed by a deep, seemingly boundless chasm, three hundred feet or more wide, with frothy edges. Nearer, with his binoculars focused on the far face, he could scarcely contain his laughter as he described disoriented schools of herring, surprised-looking dolphins, one round-eyed killer whale pop out of the vertical face and plunge into what seemed to be a flat, calm canal some one hundred feet below. The skipper of the *S.S. Hamilton* sent a radio message immediately to his owners in Seattle, where it was disregarded.

The small ketch *Blighty* out of Vancouver, crew of two, had no radio. It sailed before a gentle east wind. The owner, John Jones, dozing at the wheel, was disturbed by a gurgling noise twenty yards off the starboard bow. In the clear moonlight he saw the water frothing ahead, perhaps from the wake of a whale.

Of course, it was the brink of the swath. The *Blighty* half-slithered, plummetted, bow first in a seemingly endless plunge, as though thrown by a rogue wave, or sucked down into a maelstrom. The boat struck the level canal far below and was completely immersed for endless seconds before rising slowly to the calm surface like a half-filled bottle. The mast had snapped, the sails burst.

John Jones was tangled in his lifeline. His shipmate emerged, choking, from the waterlogged cabin where she had been asleep. They looked around themselves. They were becalmed in an endless trough between two sheer walls of water. A fish now and then plopped out of the wall near them and plunged into the level trough. The crew of the *Blighty* took it all in, and could only laugh at their predicament. Their laughter resounded through the silence of that eerie channel.

The swath entered the coast of Japan with the breaking of the dawn. Scientists from the University of Tokyo had been observing the strange behaviour of their machines, mystified by the permanence of the shock pattern. On their computers, they observed the swath track on a gentle south-west curve towards Mount Fuji. They watched from their observation towers as it gently made its mark on the Holy Mountain like the brush stroke of a Zen Master, and headed full tilt towards the city of Kyoto.

The effects of the swath on the city with its great Shinto Temples, its marvellous gardens, might be called devastating. A three-hundred-feet-wide gouge was made through the middle of the city. One hundred thousand people were simply vacuumed away.

The only inhabitants spared in its path were early morning commuters more than one hundred feet below ground in the metro
subway. They ascended decapitated escalators to find themselves
on the smooth bottom of the swath. Around them they could see
the walls of the swath, fringed by the tidy remains of the city's
skyscrapers. One of the commuters, according to news reports, a
survivor of Hiroshima who had been taking his pet pig on its first
train ride, laughed so infectiously at the sight of the swath that all
the others joined in, the pig oinked loudly, and the sounds of their
merriment filled that misty canyon.

That was the way of the swath. Despite the terrible decimation of
human life, as in Kyoto, it aroused no apparent hostility. Indeed,
early theorists presumed its benevolence. The truth is that the
swath did not mutilate any living organism, animal or vegetable.
No records exist of severe injuries, of amputations of limbs, as
might have been expected, of terrible dissections. So far as living
things were concerned, the swath took all or nothing. As for in-
animate objects, it proceeded inexorably, following an undeviating
path, dividing, obliterating, without partiality.

The swath sucked its way along the coast of South Korea, neatly
eliminating two boatloads of drowsy fishermen, but leaving intact
their bulging seine-nets in the Cheju Strait. Still maintaining its
distance ahead of the rising sun, it hissed across the Yellow Sea,
and onto the mainland of the People's Republic of China. Reports,
as always, are rather erratic from that part of the world, but it appears that in the provinces of Shensu, Szechwan, and Tsunghai,
dawn workers in paddy-fields of collective farms noticed the fren-
zied chirruping of crickets trained to warn of earthquakes. Government agencies did, however, pass on, with their official blessing, the
information that collective farm workers in their blue dungarees
heard an unfamiliar sizzle — the swath passing near, efficiently
meting out oblivion, without regard to class background.
    This swath was no respecter of national boundaries. Chinese
border guards, with a great deal of good humour it seems,
challenged it, and even fired upon its dark shadow as it eviscerated
its three-hundred-feet-wide strip from the remote territory of

Tibet, furrowing towards the walls of the forbidden city of Lhasa. The swath, at that point, seemed to be rushing at the Himalayas and the great breast of the world, Mount Everest.

Then, it changed course. The swath began to swing further west in a gentle but resolute manner.

This change of course has caused much speculation. Had the swath "achieved its goal"? (such terms are used by contemporary philosophers who study the phenomenon). Or did the invocation of certain cryptic Tibetan mystical powers divert it from its path — the screech of ten thousand prayer-wheels and monotonous chanting from the *Tibetan Book of the Dead* by innumerable devotees greet its arrival? Was the power that moved the swath deflected by the great mineral residues of the Himalayas and bent protesting in a different direction? It is, in hindsight, surprising that no one seemed to consider the swath as the other side's secret weapon. There was always difficulty in perceiving it as any kind of threat at all.

The westward wheel of the swath brought it to Tamarat in Northern India where the warrior hill-tribes were fasting for the great penitential feast of Rabakhan. In the cool dawn light, the brahmins squatted nervously on a high podium before half-a-million followers in the city square. The ritual of brahmin-hurling, an ancient rite in which the most powerful of the warriors competed in throwing a priest from the podium as far into the assembled crowds as they could, had just begun. Everyone heard the hissing sound as the swath arrived. It bored past them, removing podium and brahmins (except for one who was revolving in mid-air at the time), leaving only the tell-tale cavity behind. For a moment there was silence, then a few of the disciples began to smile, then shudders of massive laughter rocked the warrior assembly.

Who knows how the town of Darafi in Afghanistan responded to the swath's passing? The town, with its five thousand inhabitants, was sprawled along one narrow street in the swath's path. It completely vanished, leaving a few bewildered mongrel dogs and some tardy racing pigeons to investigate the canyon left behind.

Twelve hours had now passed since the swath began. There is

general agreement that this was a momentous hour in its journey. After startling the Iranian nomads at the oasis of Dasht-i-Lut during their dawn prayer (they thought it was an approaching sandstorm), the swath entered the land of Israel. It crossed the River Jordan, disposing, according to eyewitnesses, of two camels in a rowing boat in the middle of the river, swished across the Gaza Strip and plunged into the Mediterranean Sea.

Was the swath's impartial embrace of all the desert lands a miraculous symbol of Arab unification, as has been suggested by certain Muslim fundamentalists? Or was that Jewish cult (the swath spawned cults wherever it passed — even in California where it did not pass — Zoroastrian Swathists, Soka Gakkai Buddhist Swathists, Dakshincharin Hindu Swathists, Mirza Ali Swathists, and a vast selection of antinomian, homoiousian, and latitudinarian Christian millenial Swathists) right to concentrate rather on the swath's linkage of Israel and the Gaza Strip, and its complete neglect of Egypt?

Did the swath, tired and thirsty after the desert, emit a great sigh as it dipped into the Middle Sea? So certain observers with hagiographic intent have implied. At all events, for the next thousand miles the swath bored its way across that blue sea, disturbing only occasional hashish smugglers, the ghosts of Odysseus and the nymph Calypso, the long-drowned armies of a thousand internecine wars. On the small island of Pellas, however (so reliable authorities report), three naked sisters were playing a six-handed Mozart piano sonata piece on their patio in the early dawn light. Sisters, piano and island disappeared into the swath.

The swath approached the Pillars of Hercules, the gateposts of limitless ocean. Gibraltar had been evacuated, leaving only the baboons to enjoy, at last, the pristine union of rock and sea. A squadron of fighter planes was sent to reconnoitre. The boyish pilots, through the plastic hatches of their aluminum machines, were the first human beings to observe from the air, through the mellow dawn light, the swath's implacable progress as it gouged its aquatic channel. As it passed over shallows of that ancient sea, they reported that they could see seaweed-covered Atlantean columns and unbroken wine vats in wrecks of Carthaginian quinqueremes.

From a height of two thousand feet, the young pilots watched with amazement as the swath, like an archer, seemed to take careful aim, then shot right through the narrow strait into the green depths of the North Atlantic on a gentle north-westerly bearing. Their good-humoured commentary crackled over the air-waves, till they were ordered back to base.

In that dawn, the swath funnelled through the ocean just north of the mountainous Azores. By now, all the world was aware of the swath. Thousands of English and German tourists had assembled, irreverent of official cautions, on the slopes of the northern Azorean islands hoping to catch a glimpse of the wonder.

One particular group, from an international nannies' convention, chartered some local wooden whaling boats which had often faced the more orthodox perils of the deep. They rowed out towards the swath's path. All were in high spirits. They displayed, it now seems clear, that universally felt intuition that the swath "meant no harm." The swath, accordingly, swallowed the nannies to the unanimous approval of those watchers on the hills.

The great military powers, less susceptible, did not cease investigating, dispatching U2 reconnaissance planes, anti-submarine rockets, B52 bombers fitted with H-bombs, MIG 15s, photoscrutiny balloons, multiple-headed inter-continental ballistic missiles, earth-orbiting satellites, and undetectable hydrosensitive deep-sea probes.

We should not complain. Without their paranoid probings, we would lack the only visual records we have of the swath's sea passage, those fascinating, grainy films of the event. At first, in the dim light of the dawn, the camera reveals only the wrinkled face of the ocean far below. Then you become aware of something unnatural, a moving straight line bisecting the natural body of water as though drawn with a ruler.

The camer descends and the line broadens. You notice that it has depth, is actually a spectacular geometrically angled furrow through the fluid ocean. Lower still, a slight foam is perceptible at the edge of each bank. The flat calm of the "canal" itself reflects the low-flying plane like a mirror's face.

The plane containing the camera now descends below the level of the swath's banks and hurtles along between the shining sides at frightening speed. The sensation, even on film, is uncanny, as though one were travelling at enormous speed between parallel and interminable fish tanks. The walls are glassy, transparent. From close up, you see the heads of huge groupers protruding from the bank. In vain the fish try to twist themselves back: invariably they fall, writhing, into the canal below to disappear with a flick of the tail.

One particular segment of film caused much comment. The quality is imperfect, the image less than clear. It shows a great sperm whale sticking its head out of the bank and opening its vast jaws wide in astonishment. Analysts of the film are certain they can see, in the recesses of the throat of the whale, a man with a long beard and flowing robes, looking out with some curiosity at the passing plane. No explanation of this phenomenon has yet been proposed.

One of the planes arrives at the front end of the swath. At last, we can see plainly how the trough is formed in the water: it simply *appears*, full-blown, perfectly shaped, with no sensation of effort or power, no displacing of water. It is three hundred feet wide, one hundred feet deep, geometrically cornered, as though a great scoop, a great plough, a great vacuum cleaner.... No, there is no analogy, all analogies collapse beside the reality of the swath. The swath is simply there, moving relentlessly on its north-west swing. It contradicts physics and the basic laws of nature. It defies scientific understanding. It is completely convincing. The planes bear away.

The swath hissed on towards the North American coastline, in spite of a hastily organized effort to divert it by a group of psychics internationally famous for their ability to bend spoons by the powers of their minds alone. All of them testified that they could sense the aura of the swath but were quite overwhelmed (one very sensitive lady psychic swooned) by its power.

The swath seemed much more deliberate now in its progress. The whole continent awaited it. Those who were in its projected path, people who would have fled at the first warning of a hurricane, were reluctant to believe they were in any peril. They would not evacuate their houses, boats, wigwams. In fact, they showed every sign of welcoming the swath. Eyewitnesses speak of their good humour, their curiosity: "I'm really looking forward to it," was the comment on everyone's lips, as they awaited the swath's annihilating passage. Analysts have suggested that those who would not take evasive action were akin to lemmings. There were innumerable reports of suicides caused by leaping into the canyon left by the swath, or, especially, by running directly into the swath's path — as one source said, "as if to embrace a lover."

The swath penetrated the fogs off the Grand Banks and glided smoothly into the Gulf of the St Lawrence. In the dawn light, it mounted the Quebec coastline. Thousands had driven out from the little towns of the North Shore to welcome it, to watch its passing. TV cameras, microphones, photographers and newsmen from every corner of the earth assembled. Roars of approval went up, as the swath appeared, gently dissecting, calmly obliterating all before it. It *seemed* slower, but scientists say this was an illusion: the swath always kept pace with the advancing dawn. Huge flocks of sea-birds that had fed on the fish falling out of the two walls of the swath were now joined by land-birds dipping playfully in and out of the symmetrical gorge.

The swath's passage was now more like a triumphal march, a royal procession, evoking a carnival spirit, a sense of general goodwill. Its progress was stately, inexorable, a thing of beauty.

Scientists around the world had made a prediction: if the swath continued on its present course, it would arrive back at exactly the place where it began — in Trempe, Saskatchewan, twenty-four hours after it began. So it was that on a misty prairie dawn, with the sun's beams just beginning to penetrate from the east, more people than the town of Trempe had ever seen gathered to watch the swath complete its circumnavigation. They lined up on either side of its projected path as though to watch a parade. Mothers sat in lawn chairs, fathers carried babies on their shoulders so that they would have the best possible view. The excitement can only be described as intense. Helicopters warned of the swath's approach. With only a mile to go, it had definitely slowed down, so that children were able to run alongside it, and throw their candy-wrappers in its path to watch them disappear. Young men were able to play chicken by dashing in front of the swath, jumping back out of its way at the last minute. Great gales of laughter arose from the crowd when any of them would slip and disappear in its path.

At 6 A.M. exactly, as the cameras whirred, the flashes blinked, the crowd whistled and roared, the forward edge of the swath dissolved the final wafer of solid earth separating it from where it had set out twenty-four hours before. The swath was over.

A great moan arose simultaneously, recorded on innumerable recording devices. Did the sound come from the assembly of spectators who, till then, had been filled with good humour and laughter? Was it caused by the realization of some collective sense of loss? Was it the death-rattle of whatever force drove the swath itself? (Some eyewitnesses swear the sound came from *above* them.)

These questions, like all others on the nature of the swath, may never be answered. For, before we could comprehend the phenomenon we had witnessed, it reversed itself. At exactly one minute after six, whilst the sun was still rising over the eastern horizon, the great gash that scarred half the globe, instantly healed itself, the swath was erased. Buildings were reconstructed exactly as before, the land returned to its former levels, mountains had their scalps restored, rivers and oceans reverted to their previous condition (the dismasted *Blighty* found itself tossed helpless once again on the great expanse of ocean). Everything that had vanished reappeared.

Everything reappeared — except for the living things. George Ferguson, who had been trying all day to find some way of reaching his cattle across the swath, ran back to his house when he saw the restoration. He opened the door and called to his wife and sons, whistled to his dog. No response. Yet he smiled. All along the path of the swath, widows and widowers, bereaved parents and children, dog and cat owners were calling out to their lost loved ones and receiving no responses. Yet they were smiling. We used to call the missing "the victims of the swath." That was a misnomer, for we did not really regret their passing. The bereaved would smile shyly, they would sound more as if they were boasting than mourning as they recollected, "I lost my wife" (or mother or father, or son, or daughter, etc.) "in the swath, you know."

Of course, the swath encouraged speculations as to its cause: early on, people wondered if it was all a trick with mirrors that somehow went amiss. On the other hand, romantics theorized that the divine mind had fallen asleep for a moment and thus cancelled out a part of the Creation. A group that favoured inter-galactic co-operation suggested that the missing peel of earth was a kind of skin sample taken by exploring aliens, who had then returned it minus the life-forms. The theory that gained most currency, however, amongst secular humanists, was that the swath came about owing to a certain distribution of people, objects, climates (religions and races are sometimes included in the formula) which gave the impression of deliberateness to a purely mechanical oc-currence. Laboratory experiments have not so far succeeded in reproducing the swath-effect. Yet there are scientists who maintain that such a distribution of ingredients is no doubt organizing again. They have been feeding every imaginable combination of data into their computers in the hope of being able to predict the next occurrence.

The situation has changed. A year has passed and the very fact of the swath's appearance is in dispute. Witnesses are nowhere to be found, or disappear under mysterious circumstances. It is whispered that more people have gone missing since the swath than during it. I myself have received threatening phone-calls, the Office of Taxation has audited my returns for no apparent reason, and the bank has called in my loan. Many of my colleagues have been discredited, their careers in ruins. Researchers into the swath suddenly find that government records are unavailable; more and more, officialdom refers to the event as "mass hysteria."

As for us, Rowena my dear, the swath brought us together. We met, sponsored by our various universities, during that last geological dig permitted by the government, in the Rocky Moun-tain segment. We made love for the first unforgettable time where the swath began its annihilating descent towards the Pacific. You smile. You insinuate *I* caused the swath for this purpose. I smile. I disclaim any such power, I merely celebrate the miracle.

Festival

Festival

Two of us went to the festival, one came back. We took the night plane, but we didn't sleep, neither of us being great sleepers at any time, never mind on planes. Coming in over the coastline at dawn, I thought to myself, what a beautiful place, the black headlands, the long aprons of beach round green northern water, the grass and the trees greener than was possible.

"Are you all right? Are you sure you want to go through with it?"
  "I'm fine."

We took a taxi from the airport. It was ancient, and so was the driver, a man who wanted to talk. Neither of us obliged. I was tired. I wasn't in the mood for small talk, and I may have been sharp with him, or at least he stopped trying, and left us to ourselves.
  We came down from the high moorland through a gap in the hills into the outskirts of the town (we still considered it a town, though it was more of a village, a small village). The graveyard looked as though it had no new graves, just the old ghosts. We passed the first buildings on the edge of the town, run-down looking, as though no one lived in them. Then we drove past small fieldstone

houses, along deserted streets with wisps of early morning fog still lying across the lawns.

We arrived at the bigger grey granite buildings at the centre of the town, one of them the hotel. The provost had made no reservations for us (did he think we would change our minds and not come in the end?), and we were not able to find separate rooms. Even though the festival was a local affair, enough people came from the surrounding countryside to make accommodation scarce.

We slept, or tried to sleep, making the possible rigours of the festival our excuse for lying down together and not touching.

About six in the evening, we rose, ate briefly, and joined the crowds in the street walking towards the school gymnasium. The night was foggy, but not unpleasant. The children seemed impatient, but the townspeople did not hurry. They chatted to each other, and made special efforts to be polite to us. Some of them seemed to recognize us. But their avoidance of direct questions was, for me, a sure sign they knew why we were here. I thought at times I saw a glitter in their eyes, but we ourselves were excited and perhaps every one of us looked unusual.

The school gymnasium smelt like a school gymnasium. Benches on risers had been set up along the two side walls, as though we had come to watch a basketball game. Faded pennants hung from the rafters, the corners were webbed with ropes. Just inside the main doors, I could see the provost, smiling as always, a bald man with a chain of office and steel-rimmed glasses. Beside him, the school's headmaster, a youngish man who seemed a little overawed by the occasion. They greeted everyone, the headmaster paying special attention to the children, all dressed in their best clothes, unable to hide their excitement.

The provost smiled with delight when he saw us, and he shook us warmly by the hand, saying he was so glad we'd been able to accept his invitation. He knew we'd want to sit together (we didn't contradict him), and took us by our elbows to the only two wooden chairs in the entire gymnasium. As he walked us along the front of the audience, some of the crowd who were already there applauded us courteously. We sat down and he went back to his post.

"We still have time to change our minds."

"Yes. But we won't."

At seven-thirty, the seats were filled. The lights began to dim, the audience quieted down. A cluster of spotlights shone down on a circular area of the floor covered in rope mats. A small door in the wall to our right opened and a figure, hard to make out at first, moved slowly into the circle of light. She had her back to us, a young woman with waist-length jet-black hair, wearing a white house-coat tied with a cloth belt. She walked in a very self-possessed way, in spite of occasional nervous coughs amongst the audience.

In the middle of the circle, she stopped, loosened the belt and allowed her house-coat to slip from her shoulders to the mats.

She still had her back to us as she stood there, quite naked, her shoulders heaving from deep breathing. She began to turn around slowly, allowing the audience on our side to inspect her. To see her pale face. To see that her belly, dazzling white in the glare, was swollen, that her breasts bulged.

The audience was alert. The woman lowered herself gently to the mats, letting out a gasp as she lay down.

Now her breathing became loud, deep breaths, expelled noisily from her throat. "Ahh! Ahh!" For a few minutes, very regularly. "Ahh! Ahh!" Then I heard additional sounds, coming this time from the audience. "Ahh! Ahh!" All round the gymnasium, voices, soft at first, perhaps the children's, then gradually louder as the adults joined in, all of them taking up the sound. "Ahh! Ahh!" Much louder now, basses, baritones, tenors, contraltos, the fluting voices of sopranos and altos, all breathing rhythmically in time with her. "Ahh! Ahh!" Her stomach convulsing in the harsh light, deflating, puffing up. "Ahh! Ahh!" In the glare, I thought that at times the shape of her belly became geometrical, rhomboid, angular. So that I wondered, I suppose we all did, what thing was struggling inside her to be born.

The heavy breathing stopped. Now she bent her knees, opening her legs wide. From where we were sitting we could see quite clearly the pressure on her cervix. She was making a new noise now, a kind of grunting. "Uugh! Uugh!" She gyrated slowly on the mats between grunts, displaying her labour to all of the audience. "Uugh! Uugh!"

After a few minutes, the accompaniment began again. "Uugh! Uugh!" Softly, then louder. "Uugh! Uugh!" I looked around and I could hear them all now, even the bald provost, the anxious headmaster. "Uugh! Uugh!" All of them grunting in cadence. "Uugh! Uugh!" Her voice still dominating, sweat running down her face now, and her breasts. Her audience sweated with her, beads of sweat glistened on every face in that gymnasium. "Uugh! Uugh!" And now we could see the waters bursting out from between her legs. "Uugh! Uugh!" And now her vulva bulging, stretching. "Uugh! Uugh!"

She began to scream, the thin scream of a trapped rabbit. "Eeeeh!" The audience took up the scream, hardly breathing. "Eeeeh!" Her white face, her white body was gradually taking on a purple tinge, her eyes stared. "Eeeeh!" The audience screaming louder with her. "Eeeeh!" We all watched the widening vulva of the black-haired woman on the gymnasium floor, she gyrating still in spite of her pain. "Eeeeh! Eeeeh!" Letting us all see the dark circle that was forming between the brilliant thighs fringed with wet black hair. "Eeeeh! Eeeeh!" I noticed I was screaming too, we were both screaming along with her.

The woman stopped moving, stopped screaming. The creature inside her would wait no longer. The crowd watched without a sound as something slithered from inside her agony onto the mat. She too was silent now, as death. I remember we turned to each other anxiously.

What was it we all expected? I ask myself that, every now and then. A demon? A monster we were looking for? A thing each one of us had brought to that place and expected to appear before us now in the flesh? I can only testify to my own fear.

But, oh, the relief, the delight, when I saw that on the gymnasium floor lay a baby, a simple, human baby, still connected to its mother. I could have cheered with joy, as most of the children around us were cheering. We smiled at each other. We smiled, and all the audience in the gymnasium seemed to be smiling too, smiles of relief at the birth of that child.

The provost stepped forward, his chain of office glittering, his glasses sparkling in the overhead lights. He looked down at the woman. She was lying unmoving on the floor, only the rhythmic movement of her breasts showing she was not dead, in spite of the blood still oozing out of her. The little heap lay between her legs, coated in blood and mucous, no sound, its arms and legs fluttering from time to time. The provost, a pair of scissors in his hand, stooped and snipped. Then he carefully picked the baby up and held it high, turning around with it so that we could all see his trophy.

At first, silence. Then murmurs of pleasure, then shouts of "YES, YES, YES," from all round the gymnasium. I joined in, we both did, hugging each other, shaking hands with our neighbours. The baby, high in the provost's arms, steadied its head, and those eyes that had never seen opened wide and looked around the gymnasium, taking us all in.

The woman on the mats lay in her pool of blood, waiting for the afterbirth. She turned her head painfully to see what it was she had delivered. She looked up at the baby just at the very moment the baby looked down at her. On the woman's face was only weariness and pain. The baby's face became a purple wrinkle and it began to scream, and its screams could be heard above all the rejoicing in the gymnasium that night.

The hotel bar was busy after the first event. Customers shook our hands and bought us drinks. They were delighted that visitors, especially visitors like us, should have witnessed the event. It was a marvellous beginning to the festival.

"Should we, one last time?"
  "Why not?"

We could hardly wait to get away from the bar, and up the stairs to our room. We paid no attention to the damp, we threw our clothes off and fell into bed, holding each other the way we once had so long ago. We stroked each other, hugged each other, mounted each other, writhing in pleasure. And then we slept.

Hours later, I felt the chill and drew the blankets up, and we slept with arms around each other for the rest of the night.

The second night, the fog lingered still. We walked to the gymnasium with the others. For the most part they were farmers and coal-miners, with their families robust and red-cheeked, or pale and wiry. They were courteous as ever to us, but I thought I could detect more restraint than I had noticed the night before. We disagreed about that.

The gymnasium was filled by seven-thirty. Only some floodlights lit a wide strip of floor stretching between the emergency doors at each end. The provost, energetic as ever, and the headmaster, looking quite uncomfortable, walked together to the middle of the floor. They separated: the provost walked down the illuminated strip towards one set of doors, the headmaster to the other. There they turned and bowed to each other very formally. Then each pushed the doors open to the dark outside.

"Perhaps it isn't too late for us."

"Has anything changed?"

Fresh air wafted in, diluting the ingrown smell of liniment. All of us breathed gratefully and waited for the event to begin.

We didn't wait long. We heard a faint buzzing noise, distant, it might have been someone sawing down trees. The sawing noise became louder, getting nearer to the gymnasium. We looked at each other, wondering what it could be.

Then, from the open doors on our right, we noticed a black ooze spilling slowly onto the illuminated floor. The ooze was alive. It was a flood of insects spreading over the floor, its front edge straight as a ruler.

A sea with a voice. Not the buzzing we had heard a few minutes before and could still hear in the background, but a rustle, a hiss, a scuttling of papery limbs, scaly bellies on the varnished wood floor. We watched the whispering advance fearfully, alert for the tide to spill over our exposed feet.

But the insects never left the illuminated strip. The leaders were, so far as I could tell, ants and silver fish: minuscule creatures in great masses, followed by larger members of their species — speckled in colour, some of them — carrying their tiny pearls. They kept to tight formation though some of the ants would make brief forays towards the debris of popcorn, which they would portage back to the main armies without disrupting the march.

Cockroaches appeared, with bristling antennae and hairy legs we could plainly make out, millions of them, then slithering centipedes, and millipedes, some of them a foot long. We kept our feet tucked under our seats, ready to climb up on them at the slightest hint of disorder.

Yet, already, we were beginning to feel comfortable in spite of all the insects, and some of the audience were talking amongst themselves without any sense of fear. We had the feeling we were spectators at a parade, and that the insects were consciously showing off, aware of their role.

The PA system encouraged this notion by coughing suddenly to life, and a nasal voice began calling out the names of each species as it entered the gymnasium. I heard names I had never known. Bristletails, cockchafers, buffalo beetles, harlequins, sacred scarabs, stink bugs (I could see some of the children holding their noses, giggling) dung beetles, kissing bugs, stag beetles with their enormous antlers, and walkingstick bugs looking as though they'd come straight from some insect battlefield.

We could still hear the buzzing outside, getting louder in spite of the hissing in front of us and the noise of the audience. None of the insects had so far left the hall. They would reach the other exit and begin marching on the spot, so that after a while, much of the illuminated pathway was jammed up.

Now, a splintering sound filled the gymnasium. All the crickets within a hundred miles began hopping through the door in great chirruping masses. I could not help thinking they were Mexican jumping beans, leaping six feet in the air, or black flying fish skimming over a wooden ocean.

The last stragglers amongst the crickets had just made their entrance, and the entire illuminated strip of floor was full, when the buzzing noise we had heard all night exploded into the gymnasium. I put my hands over my ears to block out the pain.

Flies. Pillars of flies, twisters, cumulo-nimbuses of flies, dense fogs of flies of every kind, house-flies, black-flies, midges, horse-flies, dragon-flies, mosquitoes, obscuring the space above the crawling insects. They filled the air like inky water poured into a huge aquarium, so that the still leaping crickets would disappear up into it and drop out moments later, inverted divers. The light in the gymnasium was almost obliterated by the living, buzzing wall of flies that cut us off from the human beings on the other side.

Only about a quarter of the air space remained. In the dim light, the children cowered against their parents. They felt, as we two did, the whining presence of these flies, how they could engulf us, smother us in horror, if they once went out of control. But like the masses of crawling insects on the floor beneath them, they stayed in control, hovering in place, as though they knew exactly why they were there, the entire building vibrating with their power.

The buzzing became so loud I thought my ears would burst, even with my hands covering them. We could not speak. No ordinary human voice could have penetrated that sound. So it was that we saw, rather than heard, the entry of the bees. Bees and wasps, colourful even in the dim light, their humming causing even more vibrations, bulkier in the air than the flies, their undercarriages dangling. Platoons of them flew on the flanks of the main body, scrutinizing the audience with their multiple eyes. Behind the swarm, the vibrations were deepest, as the ponderous bodies of a million queens filled the last space above the strip, and cut off the light, like the drawing of a huge brocade curtain.

In the darkness, we all sat still, waiting. In the confined space in front of us, countless billions of insects hovered and massed, under perfect control. We were all waiting.

Suddenly, the birds were amongst them. We did not at first know they were there, snapping and gobbling. Then light appeared in the middle of the gymnasium as the insects, on the floor and in the air, divided and surged towards the two entrances, climbing over each other in their terror. I don't know how many escaped, for they crashed into a wall that devoured them, an enemy with a million mouths.

The calm nasal sound of the PA system intruded itself into the bedlam, identifying the predators. I could hear the names, and eventually could see the killers as the lights brightened: swallows, evil-looking horned larks and screamers, frenetic thrashers, swifts, goatsuckers, nightjars and nutcrackers pecking furiously at the floor, thousands of sparrows of every sort, shrikes and razorbills pouncing on the trapped crickets and bees. With their canny, greedy eyes, they were more frightening than all the monstrous-looking insects they gorged on.

In less than ten minutes it was over. The twittering of the predators stopped, as though on a signal, and they swooped out of the gymnasium. All that remained were a stunned audience and wastes of broken insect bodies, papery wings occasionally fluttering in the stark light.

For a time, no one spoke. The children were openly crying, leaning into the adults. Some people began to get to their feet and move towards the exits, carefully skirting past the heaps of bodies.

We followed the townspeople out into the cool night, no one talking, and walked back to the hotel.

Some of the usual customers were in the hotel bar, drinking quietly, with none of the previous night's joviality. I would have liked to ask them about the event, listen to them compare it with previous years. But I kept silent. We both were too busy, nursing our private dreads.

"Perhaps we could still…"
   "Stop talking about it. Please stop."

In the damp bed, we lay as rigidly apart as if a sword had been set on its edge between us. For it was a damp bed that night. The sky was full of rain, and the bedroom was chilly. That night was our last chance to talk, perhaps to agree to try again. We didn't, and there is no more to be said.

The third and last night of the festival was a clear one for that region amongst the hills. The fog had disappeared somewhere. I could see stars and a gibbous moon. We knew we were a little late as we walked along the road to the school gymnasium. The provost and the little headmaster were waiting anxiously at the door, to the background strains of music on the PA system, looking anxiously up the street towards us. They greeted us warmly. The provost took us both by the arm and spoke:

   "You still want to go through with it?"
   We both nodded.

The lights were already dimmed, and the audience was looking in our direction. The provost waved to them as he led us in. All was well.

The middle of the floor was lit by spotlights. The provost stood under the lights and spoke:

"My townspeople and my dear children. Tonight is the final night of another successful festival, and we will all see a new and very exciting event. This event takes a lot of preparation and co-operation from a lot of people, and I'd like you to join me in a big hand for everyone concerned, and especially for our two honoured guests who have travelled many thousands of miles to be involved in this event for our pleasure tonight."

He paused for the applause, then went on to explain the rules of the event to the audience. I didn't listen very carefully, I knew them only too well. Before we had accepted his invitation so many months ago we had gone over the rules many times.

He finished his speech, and the audience applauded again, and hummed with anticipation while we went to our separate changing rooms, the provost himself taking charge of me. As I walked in front of the benches, people shouted, "Good luck," "Take care," and I could almost have believed them. Someone even called out, "God bless."

The preparations were simple enough. In the changing room, I took off my coat as the provost showed me the workings of the heavy wooden-handled, single-shot pistol, letting me see the bullet already in the breach. He reminded me that each of the six members of the squad would have the same kind of pistol, but that only one of them would be loaded.

"Do they know which of them has the loaded pistol?"

"No. They draw the pistols by lot — that's part of the event."

He asked me if I wanted to go out into the schoolyard and take a few practice shots. I thanked him for his concern, but assured him that we were both excellent shots, otherwise we would never have accepted his invitation.

Through the door, we could hear the PA system blaring out dramatic music with drum rolls. The overture of the final event of the festival. There was loud applause, and I knew something was happening.

The provost opened the door a crack.

"Your friend and the rest of the squad are all ready now. Shall we?"

We walked slowly out into the gymnasium, the audience clapping. The squad was lined up in place, six of them. They were all about the same height and weight, all of them covered from head to toe in white cloaks with eye-holes cut out, and wearing white gloves and white shoes. I tried to spot the familiar shape, the stoop of the shoulders, the tilt of a head, the way the arms hung. I could not be sure.

Each of the six held a heavy wooden-handled pistol like my own.

I took my place on the mark ten yards away, facing the squad. Six shaded pairs of eyes measured me. I peered back at them, trying without success to find eyes I knew only too well.

The tension in the hall erodes my calm and my heart batters not just out of excitement, but because I know that you are one of the six facing me, that you may be the one with the deadly pistol. I take a deep breath.

The first figure raises its pistol slowly and takes aim at my head. The voice of the provost asks me the formal question:

"Do you wish to shoot?"

Surely they would not want to end the game so soon. I take my chance.

"No."

I see the finger begin to curl on the trigger, and I stand firm.

CLICK.

The hall fills with applause and the little provost nods, and smiles his congratulations to me.

After a moment, the crowd settles down again and I concentrate once more. The second member of the squad takes aim. I see the glint in the eyeholes, but not the colour, the greenness. Not the intention. Could it be your hand aiming the weapon that might mean my death? What are you thinking?

My own hand is sweating on the handle of my pistol.

"Do you wish to shoot?"

"No."

I watch with absolute clarity the gloved finger tighten on the trigger, perhaps the last thing I will ever see.

CLICK.

The right choice. The hall resounds with applause, shouts of approval. I breathe deeply.

Silence again, more sudden this time. I suppose the audience can't wait to see how the game works itself out. The squad stands unwavering, two of them now only spectators. The third member raises an arm and aims the pistol directly at my head.

I am breathing too quickly. That steady hand, those inscrutable eyes. Could this be the pistol with the bullet? Could this be you, after all we've been through together, ready to kill me with such resoluteness?

"Do you wish to shoot?"

I need time, but there is none.

"No."

CLICK.

The audience shouts with joy. I would like to breathe deeply, not this sweaty air. But the silence falls again. The fourth figure has already raised its arm, and the pistol points at my head. I must think, analyse, figure the odds. Which of the three remaining pistols will contain the bullet? My heart is thudding with excitement I have never known. I must forget about whose hand holds the weapon. I am certain now that you will not change your mind, give yourself away. I know that, like me, you will not hesitate to fire, and I love you for it.

"Do you wish to shoot?"

Instinct gives my answer.

"YES."

I raise my pistol, keeping my arm steady, and take aim. I squeeze gently, as I have so often done in practice. The pistol bucks, and the hooded figure lifts right off the floor, a brown hole appearing where the nose would have been, and the body falls backwards, the blood spurting, the pistol still snared in its hand.

The crash of the shot rings round and round and round. The stink of gunpowder overwhelms the gymnasium smells. Silence, no cheers, only the ringing in my ears. I have killed someone, but I feel nothing except that I have played the odds. I have made my choice, that part of the game is over. Now I will join all the others, a spectator. I hear my empty pistol drop to the floor.

The squad seems indifferent to the gap in its rank. The fifth figure raises its pistol.

Suddenly, I am drowning in feelings. Why, why did I fire so soon? I look towards the provost. I want to protest to him about the unfairness of the game. But I can tell nothing from his frowning face. He is too wrapped up in the game, like the crowd. I can feel their sympathies are against me. They all hope I have made a mistake, and that the bullet is in one of these last pistols. That they can enjoy another killing.

I look directly into the barrel of the pistol. My legs are weak. But I must show no fear, as we agreed. I wonder what you feel there in the squad watching me. I wonder if it is you holding the pistol. I wonder how it will feel to die.

I watch the finger tightening. I stop breathing.

CLICK.

Elation. This time, I am full of elation, alive and enjoying the game. But the audience is deadly silent, and I can't help wondering why. I have given them almost everything the game could give. We are down to the last member of the squad and my death may be seconds away. I want nothing but to get on with the game.

The pistol slowly rises in the hand of the sixth figure. There is an expertness about it that reminds me of you, when we used to practise for the festival. If only I could see the eyes. Nothing could make this moment more exciting than to know that you are the one about to fire the pistol. Please give me a signal of some kind.

The finger begins to squeeze the trigger. Will I be able to hear the blast, the first rags of sound, see the bullet winging its way towards my head, taste the metal, the shattered brain? My heart is beating wildly, I cry out.

"Is it you?"

CLICK.

Nothing has changed. Just the thud of my heartbeat, the sweaty smell of the gymnasium, the glaring lights overhead, the squad standing erect, the silence of the audience.

Vaguely I see the provost come forwards. He is not smiling. He congratulates me without enthusiasm, then murmurs that perhaps I should go now. The festival is over. The silence is disturbing, the lack of approval for my survival, the hostile faces amongst the audience, even the children's.

I drop the provost's hand and walk towards the squad, to the crumpled body on the floor, slightly on its side in a puddle of blood. The five figures still flank it, unmoving. I stoop and pull, clumsy-fingered, at the hood, tearing it away from the head. And see your hair. The hair that spills out of the hood, the fair hair, wet with blood, I have touched morning and evening all these years. The provost takes me by the arm.

I shake off his hand. The pistol. The pistol is still clutched in your gloved hand. I bend down and loosen your fingers. I slide open the breech.

The chamber of your pistol contains no bullet.

I remember leaving the village early next morning, one of those foggy mornings that are so common in the hills at that time of the year. The provost and the keeper of the hotel helped me downstairs to the taxi with my luggage. All the rest of the village was still asleep. The provost did not invite me back, as he had two years before.

We drove north, past the grey buildings on the edge of town, past the graveyard, the gravestones poking eyes in the fog. The taxi-driver was not a talkative man, but I could see how he would sneak a glance at me now and then in his rear mirror.

I did not sleep on the plane. That was something neither of us had ever been able to do.

And when I got back here, to the city, I drank a good deal. I took a long time to settle back into the humdrum life. I explained to our friends why we were no longer together, and I think, though they were shocked, they understood.

When I found out, after the last event, that all of the squad's pistols were empty, that I had the only loaded pistol, I looked at the provost and said, quite calmly, I think:

"You lied. You've made me commit murder."

He did not answer, he just looked at me. Then, in a very gentle voice, he told me that it was time to go.

Nowadays, I sleep rarely, but when I do, I sometimes dream that you are alive, and we are talking to each other. Talking, talking. Perhaps, all the long conversations we never had. And when I wake up, my eyes are wet, and I can never remember anything we said.

No Country for Old Men

No Country for Old Men

It is a Christmas party. An old man conjures up for us the bitterness of an old war, his mind penetrating the years. He remembers the wisps of trees in the dawn haze of a dale of passion. He remembers dark, rain-filled craters, seducing the war-weary to death by drowning. He remembers the trenches joining together with intricate stitchery fabrics of opposing weft. He remembers the scattering of corpses in the half-light of no man's land, arms still protecting their dead faces. He remembers the emerging shapes of hillocks of shells, innocent-seeming as heaps of canned dog food. He remembers, his eyes hollow, the echoing snap of the fixing of bayonets at dawn: our soldiers, uniformed in grey mud, suck on a last cheap cigarette. They smell the heavy smell of tobacco wafting across from the other trenches, where German soldiers puff securely on huge carved pipes, weighty as Mausers.

"All dead now. All losers in the long run."

He says this without a smile. We listen intently.

"My own life is a miracle. Feel here. Feel the shrapnel? It floats around in my flesh like bits of broken eggshell in the white of an egg. Notice how I stoop to draw breath? Mustard gas, inhaled sixty years ago."

The old man speaks of one regret. We are all ears.

"Of those I killed, I remember clearly only one German soldier, a boy as young as myself. I was on sentry duty on Christmas day. I woke from a doze and found him leaning over me in his alien helmet. His hand was reaching into his kitbag. I stabbed upwards, as I had been taught, thrusting till I saw the blood appear on his lips. I pulled down. The blood drained along the bayonet's gutter neatly, as it should. As he fell, his kitbag spilled out a bottle of wine and a loaf of white bread. Too late, my comrades came running to tell me there was a Christmas truce amongst us, no war for the day. We hid the murdered soldier so that they would not stop bringing the wine and the bread."

That is the old man's regret. Now he means to tell us of a dream. We listen urgently.

"For the last seven nights I have dreamt of that murder. I see myself back in the trenches, the German soldier leaning over me. I know what I must do. I jab the bayonet up into his stomach, holding it till I see the blood at his lips. I pull down, noticing how neatly the blood drains along the bayonet's gutter. Then I step back from the body, and I am in my study. I walk to my desk and open the right-hand drawer. I carefully place the bloody bayonet on top of a sheaf of notepaper, close the drawer, and go back to bed. I have dreamt this for seven nights. On six of the mornings when I awoke, I went to the desk drawer to check, just in case. Only the blank paper confronted me. But this morning, Christmas morning, something was not the same. Even after I awoke, I could still feel the chill of the trenches in my bones, I could remember the weight of the bayonet in my hand. I arose, aware of the beat of my heart. The light of the first snowfall reflected into my study. I walked towards the desk: this time I had no doubt I would find in it the bayonet, on a sheet of blood-stained paper. I gripped the handle of the drawer firmly and wrenched it open. I found nothing. Just a sheaf of clean white paper as before. No miracle had happened. I was the same as other men. I could not cheat a nightmare, steal a part of it, smuggle it into the waking world. Was I not foolish to think that I would find in my desk the bayonet from my dream?"

He appeals to us, his face tired, his eyes pleading. We are ready to forgive anything. Then a grave young man I do not know stands up from amongst the group of listeners. He speaks quietly, his voice compelling. We make a circle round him.

"Last night I dreamt about a Christmas party. In the dream, one of the guests, an old man whose face I cannot remember, tells a group of people (I am one of them) how he murdered a German soldier on a Christmas day long ago. He says he is haunted by a nightmare in which he commits the murder over again, and that he has tried to end it by bringing the weapon out of the nightmare, without success. He begs for pity. The party finishes, and in my dream I follow him to his home. It is snowing. He enters his house. I watch over his shoulder as he bends over the desk in his study. He slides open the right-hand drawer. There, on a sheaf of stained paper, lies a black-handled bayonet. The old man reaches into the drawer and slowly raises the blade, still red with the blood of the victim, to his own red lips. After that I awoke."

Now his eyes are burning as he stares at the old man. The old man lowers his head before us all. He stands still, makes no appeal, for he knows there is no forgiveness in us.

A Train of Gardens
Part I: Ireneus Fludd

A Train of Gardens
Part I: Ireneus Fludd

We wait beside the Seventh Car of the Train of Gardens. Even if
Ireneus Fludd emerged, right now, many of us would not know
him. We have never met him in person. Nor is it easy to picture
him, for there are so many varying descriptions of him. He is one
of those who can undermine words. He has been called — for he
has had his share of criticisms — "lank," "a pygmy in physique," "a
lump-sack," "a bone-bag," "mister macho," "listless as a lettuce."
Otherwise reliable observers are of little help: they speak of "that
inimitable voice," "that studied reticence," "that bulbous nose,"
"those aquiline features," "that fiery diadem of orange hair," "that
reptilian poll," "that honest laugh," "that insinuating snigger." It is
not easy to picture so motley a man ("Frenchified," they say, or
"Hebraic," "Mongolian in feature," "your pint-of-Guinness Dublin
looby"). Yet we persist in the hope of seeing him with our own eyes,
here at the exit of the Train of Gardens.

"He hasn't come out yet?" we ask.

No answer. None is needed. The morning sky is brilliant, and
some of the group have loitered here all night. Is this, then, what it
has all come to? Is this the end of the discoverer of the secrets of
Oluba? We cluster, his admirers, uneasy beside the Seventh Car of

the Train of Gardens. We, remembering, are not willing, as yet, to surrender to grief.

oozed onto cloth of silk

We wait beside the Seventh Car of the Train of Gardens. Will Ireneus Fludd ever emerge? We, his admirers, may never know the secret of his youth, only the rumours, only the insinuations that have so readily been embraced by his enemies. I think of the claims of Alfredo Florentino, erudite son of an ecclesiastical brickmaker. Florentino avowed to a newspaper reporter that in the past he knew Fludd (Fludd acknowledged this only with reluctance). Florentino, hawking up brick-red phlegm in his brickyard in Venice, declared that Fludd once confided to him the great trauma of his early life: the memory of his alarming ride, slide, along the chute of the natal canyon. Florentino, a man who prided himself on exactness of recall, spat neatly, perhaps without malice, and recalled:

"He said he experienced a state, then a state, then a state: comfort, security, warmth. Then a state and another state: discomfort, pain. Then three things: a squeezing of the skull, a feeling of being sucked through the insides of a monster worm, then a short drop into noise and cold." To Florentino, Fludd sounded Italian, rolling his r's, spitting out his t's with Latin aggression. Florentino's own red spit dribbles down his black beard.

(Fludd has always hinted darkly that he cultivated the Italian mannerism for a time to allay suspicions, conceal himself from his critics: all his life he has known there would be certain unspecified forces hostile to someone like him.)

Florentino said that Fludd even described his natal bed:

"Five things he told me about that bed, that room: a four-poster, he said that bed was, with blue curtains around it. A *camera da letta*, he said that room was, very beautiful, with windows, he said, looking onto a garden full of lilies at one end. A maze, he said, a maze of privets at the other." Florentino, coughing violently, had accused Fludd to his face of being an aristocrat. Fludd had sighed at the charge, regretting Florentino's persistence. "The oak understands the axe," he liked to say.

the frangipani mourns

Those Oluban findings should have astonished the world. Those Oluban findings did nothing of the kind. Instead, because of his unorthodox methods, his lack of footnotes, they cost Fludd all intellectual respectability. He did not mind. The Oluban phase came at a time (he was then twenty-five) when he was dissatisfied with received opinion and felt that he must personally re-examine certain aspects of human behaviour. As always, despite his lack of formal training, he pursued his goals with the utmost rigour. The results were remarkable.

He chose as his operational base a remote South Pacific island called Oluba. To protect the island, Fludd says, from marauding anthropologists, he will not give its exact geographic location. He reveals only that it lies at the western extremity of the New Caledonia group. He flew to Queensland, Australia, in February. From there, he took a berth on a fishing schooner bound for the islands. It was the cyclone season, but nothing could dampen his excitement and his sense that a great spiritual adventure was under way.

The journey was rough (they say he mutters about "mutinies," "keel-hauling," "force tens," "great white sharks," "the cat-o'nine-tails"), but eventually the ship thundered through the perilous entrance of a reef into a translucent lagoon, and he beheld the island of his hopes, Oluba. Steamy Oluba. "A teeming carbuncular eruption in a soupy ocean," according to Fludd, in a poetic moment. Oluba, clamorous with fertility and energy.

It was on this island that he encountered that Oluban hallucinogen, the ineffable *sarga*. (He learnt its secrets from a native girl, Watonobe; she it was, too, who introduced him to the bizarre sexual practices of the islanders.) On Oluba, all the males are expected to eat the *sarga*, which is a product of the hormone of the red sponge-fish peculiar to the island's reef.

The account that follows is a transcription of Fludd's unpublished manuscript, which, in spite of attacks upon its veracity by academics, has enjoyed a cult following for its description of the *sarga* customs and for its analysis of his sexual initiation on Oluba. He intends to revise his manuscript for publication and to answer scholarly criticisms, after the Train of Gardens project. Here it is as he left it.

Oluban male children eat *sarga* whilst they suck the mother's milk. They eat a quantity daily till they arrive at their sixteenth copra harvest. At that age, the young males prepare, for the first time, to join with the veteran devotees, and *ratinake* ("pay the price") for the *sarga*, to which they are completely addicted. The price is a very severe one. In exchange for continued access to the drug, they must sacrifice, annually, in advance, one of their limbs.

I am the only outsider ever to have observed the ceremony (this came of my friendship with Watonobe), and only on one occasion. It was at the end of March. For weeks there had been an aura of unhealthy excitement all over the island. Even the dogs were nervous, and not merely because of the cyclone season, humid and overcast.

On the evening when the ritual was to be performed, the drums began pulsing at six o'clock as the stormy sun sank into the rough sea. Bonfires lit up the central gathering place where all the islanders assembled. There was no sign of their habitual joyousness on their faces.

Suddenly the drums reached fever pitch and into the middle of the arena leapt a huge naked female figure wearing a vivid devil mask. Her body glistened with sweat as she danced, the coronas of her great breasts rolling wildly like extra eyes. This was the high priestess of the cult of the *sarga*. She lurched to a halt and the drumming ceased.

And now, into the firelight, the devotees walked, hobbled, or were carried by the young boys who were about to *ratinake* for the first time. I have never seen such a collection of maimed bodies: it was worse than any photograph showing the aftermath of trench warfare. Aside from the novices, who were still intact, even the younger devotees already lacked noses, or ears or eyes, or fingers, or toes. The older men were proportionately more mutilated: an arm, a leg or two might be gone.

Last came a small group of disciples, carrying on a litter an elderly man, who had managed to reach *Otusuna*, "The Thirty-One Years." For him the sacrifice had now become a deadly one. The name, "The Thirty-One Years," came from the traditional Oluban theory that a man has thirty-one expendable external parts (ten fingers, ten toes, two arms, two legs, two eyes, two ears, a nose, a tongue, a penis — which, with the testes, the Olubans regard as a unit). Few men survive the amputation of all thirty-one, retaining only the internal organs of their stumps of bodies.

The amputations of the younger men's limbs began on a slab of rock in the middle of that arena. Let me say only that the butchery was performed with great dexterity by the priestess and her assistants, who were soon smeared with blood. The sand around them was stained with blood. Blood congealed and dripped from that stone slab like candlewax from a great squat candle. The victims gave themselves willingly, many of them uttering no sound of pain, even when their wounds were cauterized in hot tar. They were cheered wildly by the Olubans according to the extent of their sacrifice. Special applause greeted the neophytes, whose families looked on with pride.

But a great hush came over them when the turns came, at last, of those who had little left to give, the ascetics who lived almost solely on *sarga* and water, who hummed constantly a tongueless monotone, and were in perpetual ecstasy. That huge priestess's knife might now be the instrument of their deaths.

Watonobe, clutching my arm tightly, whispered that among the *Thirty-Oners*, those who have retained their penises till last are revered by the women of Oluba and it is considered a great honour to be allowed to sleep with one of them. In such cases the disciples will lay the saintly devotee on top of the woman so honoured, and act as his missing limbs. They will join the two bodies in a sexual union and discreetly rock the man back and forth, back and forth, gently increasing the momentum till, by the quality of his humming, they sense that orgasm is imminent. A few moments later, after a signal from the woman, they will detach the *Thirty-Oner*, and carry him away looking, as Watonobe said, for all the world like a long-spouted teapot without a handle.

Young girls plead to be given to these terminal devotees for sexual initiation, and if they are lucky enough to conceive a child, it is treasured, and known as *erace* ("nearest to the gods"). Watonobe told me with pride that she herself was *erace*.

The elderly man I had seen earlier was the last to be brought to the altar. His name was Baratee. The islanders crushed forward to brush his body with their finger-tips as he was carried to the stone. Horribly maimed as he was, he had retained his penis, nor did he intend to part with it now. He had communicated to his disciples that he wished instead to forfeit his heart.

A great sigh arose from the assembly when they heard this. As Baratee was laid upon the altar, he hummed his cheerful monotone. He hummed on for a time, then, still humming, nodded his eyeless, earless, noseless head. The priestess plunged the knife into his chest. The humming stopped. In the profound silence, she excavated the heart, and raised it in the air, the blood dripping onto the body which still twitched nervously on the stone of sacrifice.

That was the end of the ritual. The Olubans now turned to feasting and dancing, rejoicing over the death of Baratee. His body was to be boiled and fragments of it distributed as relics amongst the islanders.

Scholars may be interested to note that not all devotees of the *sarga* persist in their dedication. Some have escaped its charms after losing only a few limbs. They are looked on as apostates, or feeble-minded.

"Look how they treat me," one of them told me, "I must help harvest the copra" (an act of self-pollution for a male in Oluba), "I am forbidden entry into the village, they will not allow me to play with the children. Only the most destitute of the prostitutes will entertain me. Didn't I give up enough? Look at my ears, look at these fingers."

Even lower in regard are the males who refused to sacrifice any limbs at all. They carry the scars of their wholeness with them, and not even the prostitutes will associate with them. They are violent men prone to suicide and bestiality.

That is how the first part of the manuscript ends. "Ah! the whiteness of the leper," Fludd would often comment to those of his disciples who read the segment, "the whiteness of the leper is the only true whiteness."

phalanxes of immortals

Fludd has allowed us to read his unpublished manuscript on the myth-making powers of the Olubans. The subject was clearly of great interest to him (it is a little too iconoclastic for some of his critics). A brief summary shows its general directions.

To begin with, Fludd tries to impress Watonobe with the variety of gods in the world he has come from. He names their sacred names: Jupiter Fulgur, Orcus, Agdistes; Heindall and Frigg; Morrigan and Grobniu; Sarasvati and Avalokitesvera; Jagannath and Narsinh; Amen-Ra and Thoth; Ereshkigal and Upnapishtim; Amatsumar and Ninigino-Mikoto; Changs and Wangs innumerable.

She hears him out and laughs. She tells him something he can hardly conceive of: Oluba is an incubator of cosmogonies. Each Oluban family invents its own creation myth, vying with the others in originality, splendour, vulgarity. To convince him, Watonobe introduces Fludd into the longhouses at full moon, the myth-telling period.

He visits the Makibo family longhouse and hears their family myth told by Amra the loud, happy minstrel-aunt. Between sucks on her pipe, she sings of the self-indulgent deity, Butobo, who overeats then defecates and vomits into the void, forming the stars, the planets, the Milky Way. The ocean on which Oluba floats is Butobo's almighty urine, the island itself a marvellous turd on which his parasites, the Olubans, grow. Amra the minstrel supplies the sounds of Butobo's exertions so realistically that the audience is filled with wonder.

In his visits to the other longhouses, Fludd makes notes on countless creators. A creator who lives in two-syllable words. A creator who is suffering from the Oluban equivalent of a nervous breakdown. A creator who, like a coral snake, casts off his skin with each millenium, every skin becoming a new world. A creator whose sleep must never be disturbed, for this world is a dream of his. A creator who has made the world so perfect he envies it and wishes to annihilate it. A creator who didn't really make this world, but came into possession of it through a potlatch with a demon, its real maker. A creator who created the world so that it might enjoy *sarga* forever. A creator who made life by accident through pronouncing the wrong spell, and who must be prevented from finding a counter-charm. A creator who is afraid to reveal himself to his creation because he cannot live up to its image of him....

Watonobe's own family myth delights Fludd. She herself was conceived on the last night of the life of her father, Simpe (a legend on the island), a "*Thirty-Oner*," who had died upon removal of his penis. He had composed the myth before losing his ability to communicate, and Fludd now hears it sung by Watonobe's mother, Panua.

This creator is named Rampa, the sexual power. He controls a vast ("a million times a million") harem of sex-goddesses, with whom he consorts infinitely, inventing a myriad love-techniques, some of which survive only on Oluba. Rampa is at the heart of all creation. When he observes an earthly man and woman make love, Rampa mates simultaneously with one of his goddesses. He then miraculously transplants the divinely fertilized egg into the womb of the earthly mother. He is thus truly the father of the human race, and is kept very busy.

The only rite he insists upon is the act of love itself, which gives him supreme joy. Watonobe's family is not remiss in its observation, as Fludd is soon to discover. In later years, he will repeat to his disciples with approval the pithy Oluban proverb, "many gods, few sins."

behold the waters
We wait beside the Seventh Car of the Train of Gardens. We stand here thinking now about the hands, the feet of Ireneus Fludd. His hands and feet occupy us, because of a version of the first eighteen years of his life that has been widely circulated. The source is a broadsheet by Fortescue and Perdonta de Medullin, brother and sister, bachelor and spinster, amateur ichthyologists, joint Elders of the Church of Reformed Morals, and renowned ascetics. The de Medullins, prolific authors of admonitory broadsheets and pamphlets on the ethical behaviour of fish, have loudly condemned

Fludd as a liar, a pervert and a corrupter of fish. They claim to
have known Fludd's parents (Fludd has denied the claim vigorous-
ly). In a broadsheet entitled *Leviathan in a Goldfishbowl*, the
de Medullins take turns in proclaiming their version of Fludd's
youth to the world. The first part is written by Fortescue, the
cosmopolitan *par excellence*, who has been hounded out of every
country in Europe and Asia, and incorporates a number of their
linguistic peculiarities into what he calls his "universal voice of
prophecy." He begins:

> The person, "Ireneus Fludd," is a creature of the most un-
> natural. Not is this suggesting he is of entirely to blame. Con-
> sider to this background. His father, which the name of I am
> sworn to conceal (such is his depraved the conduct, one is
> understanding his desire at anonymity) was a professorial of
> Biology at the Sorbonne. His mother, a most moral weakling,
> became all pregnant, and feared the carry of her child, for it
> might in her inside have an explosion. Sparing to her, *M le Pro-
> fesseur* debagged the foetus at her womb and transferring did
> into a construction plastic womb.
>
> Oh! sadly, sadly! The foetus insettled down to it, unfor-
> tunately if I may so say it for the world, to grow at quite a
> health. After the nine months having been so passed to the
> fulness, it was for born urgency.
>
> But now, *M le Professeur* and the so moral weakling wife
> wanted the preference of being expecting the baby, not having
> one not actually. They much desired the need to keep him in
> the plastic womb the longer more awhile. Renovations of such
> plannings were needed. Enlarge the womb was done, a liquid
> thousand of liters pumped over, and glassy windows made this
> womb a plastic so to be like a tank of very fish.

At this point in the pamphlet, the hand of the sister, Perdonta,
takes over:

> You can imagine the warped pleasure of the parents when
> their spawn made his first tentative breast strokes into the
> annex of that artificial womb. Now they could watch the

monster's daily growth. They saw his reddish-black bristles begin to sprout, the blue-green eyes exploring his watery world. The infamous parents pursued their abominable course to its end. They gradually introduced into the tank, to keep him company, instead of teddy-bears and toy cars, a variety of cold-blooded companions. They surrounded him with kissing gouramis, loach gobies, intemperate basses, a croaker or two, a disgusting goatfish, some porgies, some irresponsible black pomfrets and flagtails, a quota of halfmoons and moronic bonnetmouths, five sand stargazers, two three fin blennies and a graveldiver. Fitting company for such a child! They were all as corrupt in the end.

The baby, however, was curious about the creatures outside his tank, forever spying upon him, and soon began to recognize them. He would swim over to meet his parents accompanied by the other fish who accepted him, because of his strangeness, as their natural leader. The fiendish parents would call out, "Ireneus! Come, Ireneus!" and his lips would bubble intuitively the words, "da-da," "ma-ma."

They hired a Scottish nanny with the kind of debauched past that assured her co-operation to see to the needs of their son. She taught him to read, holding up the alphabet books to his inhuman eyes. The conniving witch would press her lips against the glass and shout words. He would gurgle them back to her till the tank reverberated with their grotesque communications.

The remainder of Fortescue and Perdonta de Medullin's tale is predictable: one day, many years later (Fludd was now eighteen), a beautiful female student of *M le Professeur*'s, a *Mlle* Madeleine de Rocheau, inadvertently entered the tank-room and gazed at the lily-white youth, still harnessed to his umbilical cord. Fludd swam to the window of his tank, and gazed back at her in astonishment. Till that moment, he had experienced undefined longings only for a sleek amberjack, or an aloof papagallo. Now, for the first time, he felt a swelling in the area of his genitalia, in which the *mademoiselle* was showing an interest. Clutching himself, he kick-stroked awkwardly to the opaque part of the tank. The water seethed. A moment later, filaments of a milky substance drifted like mermaid's ribbons before the eyes of the curious *mademoiselle*.

That night, Ireneus Fludd asked *M le Professeur* to release him, to let him at last be born.

A few hours afterwards, he who for eighteen years had breathed only under water gulped down his first shock of air. He who had touched only the cold scales of his fish friends felt for the first time the warmth of human contact. He who could swim as expertly as a dolphin made his first terrifying efforts to walk upright. He who had only gargled the soliloquies of Shakespeare, the lyrics of Tennyson, spoke for the first time, a burbling Scottish twang like his nanny's.

He heard his own voice with amazement.

This is the de Medullins' version of the early years. Some of Fludd's former friends say that he does have webbed fingers and toes (he tries, they say, always to keep them covered, insists on mittens, will not wear sandals). They say he will gaze longingly at an oceanscape. They say he will visit only cities with aquaria, and prefers to socialize only with friends who have fish-bowls in their homes. They say when he approaches a bowl, the fish congregate by him, and that he has often spent whole evenings staring at them with dilated eyes, making peculiar lippy noises.

Fludd, on the other hand, has only one word for the de Medullins: "charlatans." Yet he will often say to his disciples, "Consort not with the darkness of waters," and he will smile enigmatically.

sneaked into innocence

Watonobe, Watonobe. The name chimes all through the Oluban papers of Ireneus Fludd, sometimes doodled sensuously in the margins. She attached herself to him, though as a rule Oluban women scorned unmutilated males. Fludd's deviance was overlooked, a foreigner's eccentricity. Many of us have seen that remarkable though incomplete manuscript dealing with her sexual tutelage of Fludd. Though professional anthropologists have (for their own reasons) rejected the whole document as utterly specious, he regarded this tract as of primary importance, and meant to give it his full attention when he put his affairs in order.

Some of the terms are still in their original Oluban form:

Watonobe intended me to be her *unor* ("student") in the Oluban way. She was beautiful, her eyes were ageless. Like all Oluban beauties, she had great muscular thighs, which she constantly exercised by flexing and knee-bends. She had spent the years since her twelfth copra-harvest in perfecting the love methods of *ana pria* ("ways of loving"). She would refer to her many previous *unors* as a scholar acknowledges some authority. Her frankness disconcerted me at first, though I was aware she was simply displaying her credentials as a tutor. That first night's lesson was unforgettable, the moon over the lagoon, the breakers distant and soothing. The air was full of spice and flowers.

Watonobe began by coaxing me to the longhut to chat with her mother and the rest of her sisters. I felt a little awkward as she told them that I was to be her *unor*. They laughed knowingly, and said they'd learn all the details of the lesson from her in the morning. Her mother, Panua, still an exotic creature herself, more like an elder sister, massaged Watonobe's neck and shoulders with *santra*-oil, an absolute pre-requisite for love-making on Oluba.

Then Watonobe and I bade them good night, and walked hand in hand to the little hut dedicated to such *ana pria cuna* activities. Thus began a night, the first of many I spent on Oluba, which I shall never forget.

We entered the hut. Slowly, without any shyness, she unfastened her sarong and allowed it to slip down to the rattan floor. Then she undid my shirt, and peeled it slowly from me. Then my trousers. As she undid the zip, I could feel her cool fingers slide along my *umpum*.

Despite my efforts to remain calm and observant, I was becoming excited. She took my head in her soft hands and gently pressed it to her scented body, my face against her swelling *zumbas*. We lay down together, she above me. And now she began to kiss me, gradually moving her warm lips down my body, until I felt their moistness brush my *bagu*. Her fingers began the soft caress known as *iserime*, which ensures that passion does not come to a head prematurely. And now, still fondling *umpum* and *olbolu*, she lay beside me so that I might admire her magnificent body.

As a courtesy to my teacher, and so that I might learn more about these Oluban practices, I took a deep breath and kissed her neck and shoulders, adjusting my body so that she did not need to interrupt her caresses. Soon I was kissing her magnificent *zumbas*, noting all the time the coloration and texture of the upright *atitas*.

She also was beginning to breathe more quickly and utter signs of contentment, as I intuitively continued the exploratory path with my tongue. Her palpitating *ulavula* loomed before me, exuding the most exotic odours and my tongue probed it much to her delight.

Then suddenly, forgetting for a brief moment all my scientific objectivity, I lunged at that incredibly well-developed *nimpaclic*.

Now she began to squirm as we both, she with her trembling, no-longer-cool fingers, I with my earnest tongue, continued our lesson.

I fully realize that a scholar might well object to all of this. He might complain that these practices are in no way particular to Oluba; they are the common-or-garden stock-in-trade of lovers the world over. I acknowledge the validity of the point. Bear with me.

For now began my initiation into the unique carnal rites of Oluba. During one of my manoeuvres, Watonobe uttered a delirious squeal, and the door of the hut burst open. In came running her mother, the comely Panua, and her two sisters, Carama and Anata. They were all as beautiful as Watonobe, with their shining dark brown hair and delightful features. Imagine my curiosity when all three, laughing with joy, threw off their sarongs, and joined us on the rattan floor, grasping and fondling parts of my body in the most titillating way. I was totally immersed in *zumbas*, all fragrant with the most beautiful of odours, whilst my own *umpum* and *olbolu* were constantly and variously manipulated.

This was surely the most mystical of sensual experiences: I

entered into an unparallelled divine unity with the four, all of whom devoted their energies to my compliant flesh.

Watonobe had no sooner coaxed my throbbing *umpum* into her *ulavula* than I felt a moist pressure behind me in the area of my *asana*. It was the gorgeous sister, Carama, whose tongue was delicately probing whilst her elegant fingers were dandling my *bagu*. As if this were not enough, that other delightful sister, Anata, stood over me, spread her legs, and descended upon my face from above, inviting me to insert my tongue into her own moist and odorous *ulavula*. This unlooked-for familial hospitality to a stranger touched my heart. All the while, the maternal Panua encouraged her daughters to do their duty, delicately adjusting limbs, wiping untimely spills, or excessive perspiration, with a sandalwood sponge.

My nerves were tingling with such pleasure, in spite of my efforts to maintain a scholarly perspective, that Panua would occasionally *rumubumu* me in a certain way, and by uncanny skill, prevent my too early *lodawe*.

Yet the moment surely could not be delayed much longer, for I was ready to discharge, regardless of her technical skills. Panua clapped her hands, and suddenly, outside the hut, a bevy of drums began to beat a pulsating, driving rhythm. "Now is the time for *meniveni*," Panua whispered, "at last! at last!"

A dozen other beautiful Oluban women dashed into the hut, and they too fell to the rattan floor. They began stimulating each other with great energy and laughter till the floor was moist with their activity, for they administered *rumubumu* and *iserime* to whichever body was nearest, including, especially, my own.

I had never witnessed such acts of selfless devotion; my heart was thudding to the drum-beat, though I made every effort to maintain my academic detachment. The most curious part of the entire evening was still to come, however. Now Panua took Watonobe by the hand and led her towards a horizontal bamboo pole suspended about five feet above the floor. She helped my athletic instructress to leap up to the bar, and hang there by the knees, her legs apart, her head downwards, her long raven hair trailing on the rattan mat. Watonobe was looking at me from her upside-down position, calling to me, extending her arms towards me. At first I was quite at a loss, then the realization of what I was expected to do dawned upon me. Panua and the others, smiling with pleasure and anticipation, led me to her. They gently turned me upside down too, and with great expertise, hoisted me into the air and slotted my *umpum* neatly into the open, glistening *ulavula* of my teacher. Then they let go of me. We hung there like a left-over clothes-peg on a line. At first I was mortally afraid of injuring myself, and clung desperately to Watonobe. She wrapped her arms around me with pleasure, and now I under-stood why these women had developed their quadraceps so highly. She was able to take the weight of both of us with ease, and began to make scissoring movements with her thighs. Never have I experienced such bliss. Watonobe was squealing with pleasure as we embraced upside down, like mating bats, or trapeze artists at a private orgy. Our audience looked on with smiling faces, then continued their own activities. Every-where, I could see nothing but *atitas*, *ulavulas*, *zumbas* abound-ing, a frenzy of *rumubumu*, *iserime*, *meniveni*, *nimpaclic*, and *lodawe*, *lodawe*, *lodawe*, until I cried out, "Dear Heavens!"

Here the manuscript peters out. Fludd planned to complete it and render into appropriate English the rather obscure technical jargon after the Train of Gardens project.

We are aware of the importance of the Oluban period to Fludd. He saw in that remote island society glimmerings of a truth which he would express to his disciples in his most profound dictum: "The rule of the imagination over the senses is the only key to human happiness."

His Oluban researches have been rejected, of course, by profes-sional academics. He came to feel that, by "originality," what they really mean is the invention of ingenious ways to support outmod-ed ideas. Fludd never lost confidence in his own vision, which he would embody ultimately in his ineffable Train of Gardens.

A Train of Gardens
Part II: The Machine

A Train of Gardens
Part II: The Machine

We wait beside this Train of Gardens glistening in the morning sun, the masterwork of Ireneus Fludd. The plan for it matured during one of his philanthropic periods. He had considered building a fleet of mobile swimming pools using cast-off oil-tanks, in which, on sultry days of summer, the city's ghetto-children might dip themselves.

He forsook this idea for the appeal of a grander scheme: a Train of Gardens. He would construct a travelling Botanical Gardens to bring the true splendours of nature into every city, town, village, hamlet of North America, South America, Europe, Asia. THE WORLD.

Yes, his ambition grew, and so did the conception: his Train of Gardens must be the great experience in the lives of all who entered. It must be that perfection of nature he had always desired. He would fit his Train with adjustable wheels to bring all the world within its reach: already he saw it teetering along narrow rails through the outback of Australia, skirting the white beaches of Fiji, the barren moors of the Aleutian Islands. He saw his Train steaming along the volcanic ridges of the Tuamotu Archipelago and the Marquesas, flouting the mountain winds and glaciers of

Tierra del Fuego and Greenland. He saw it chugging along the toy tracks of the sugar-cane fields of Trinidad, the bogey-rails of the coalfields of Central Scotland.

Fludd's plan was and is prodigious. Here stands the Train, a great steam-engine, at rest now, shackled to seven rebuilt freight cars with thick glass roofs. In each car, an episode of the Train of Gardens.

Three weeks ago on this day, a sunny morning, Ireneus Fludd entered the First Car, began his journey. He would be the first human being to travel through to the Seventh Car. It was an enterprise for which he had been preparing all his life.

The First Car
the north woods. Fludd immediately encounters the dark walls of green forest on all sides. He steps precariously on pine needles, their scent rising to him. The woods are silent, restful, no cry of a bird. Now he breaks into a clearing, now he sees a fragment of sky, an eagle, its prey dangling, sloping towards its eyrie. He comes upon tracks. He sniffs the air. He smells the stink of bear. He stiffens, on guard. Does he glimpse a malevolent face? Mad eyes assessing him from a thicket? She moves out from behind a huge pine tree, a black-haired woman of great beauty, in a green robe, innocent blue eyes surveying him. She smiles and slowly unbuttons the front of her robe, her golden breasts welling out before him. She smiles. He begins to speak. Each word, like a blow, beats her down. She crouches, then swells, matted hair covers her face, her body. Fangs protrude from her snout. She growls deeply, reaches towards him with scything claws. He stumbles from her, runs as fast as he can, runs, runs endlessly. "In the body of the beast dwells pleasure," Fludd tells himself, as he runs.

The Second Car
the river. A torrent is sucked through the groins of a ravine. Fludd embarks in a wooden canoe. The current snatches him along. White foam, shredded by black rocks, flies everywhere. Whirlpools pock the surface entrapping the unwary. Fludd, exhilarated by the speed and danger, holds on tightly to the spar of his canoe. His arms ache, he is chilled to the bone. She appears straddling a slick

black rock in the middle of a swollen section of the river. She is naked, her body, her red hair, glistening in the spray. She is slowly rubbing herself on the smooth finger of rock. She opens her arms to
welcome him to her. Her beauty overcomes him. He smiles, and
she disintegrates. That beautiful body turns gelid and formless.
That face is disfigured by warts and wrinkles. Like a great toad she
slides into the water towards him. No path leads up those walls
fringed far above by bushes. Sometimes a boulder plunges down,
as though deliberately aimed, almost striking the canoe. "Beware
lest you drown in the spirit," Fludd tells himself. He hears the
plunging of the beast in the water behind him.

The Third Car

the mountain. The only route lies through a high pass of unearthly
beauty. Cold numbs his body, avalanches constantly threaten. The
rock-face climb taxes even Fludd's skill. Pitons and axes are the only
help in that cruel place. Ropes dangle ready in position, but he
knows they are not to be trusted, for he can see they have been partly sawn through. He hears a crunching in the snow just below him.
She stands there, looking up at him, more beautiful than ever,
wearing a white smock, flowers in her golden hair. In that frigid air,
she caresses her breasts through the flimsy dress, slides her long
fingers between her thighs, looking at him. There is no resisting
her smile. He stoops to help her up, raises her cool white hand to
his lips. The flesh sears, and he looks into the insane eyes of a wolf,
burning eyes, the smell of putrid flesh in the air. He tears himself
away and climbs on, with urgency. Fierce winds wrench at him on
the ice face, threatening to plunge him into the abyss. The ice
cracks terrifyingly around him. In the dark and the cold, he knows
he must bivouac in an ice cave and await the ferocious dawn. He
lies, shivering, waiting, hearing inhuman howls from outside. "Ascend ye therefore to unknown valleys," Fludd tells himself.

The Fourth Car

the ocean. It shimmers at the foot of the mountains. The water
sparkles so clear that Fludd can see fish flicking around on the bottom. A fisherman's empty sailboat waits on the white beach. On the
distant horizon squats the outline of a coast. He pushes the boat

gently into the swell, raises the sail, lowers the centreboard, grasps the tiller, and bears away westwards. Now the sea changes its mood. The sky darkens, a whistling offshore wind and driving rain assail him. No hope remains of beating back to that haven in this flimsy craft. The wind turns to gale-force, batters the tiny hull, rogue waves threaten at any moment to breach or pitchpole the vessel. Off his port quarter a black sailboat rapidly approaches. She stands in the bow, clutching the foremast. Her robe is completely open, billowing like a cloud, and he sees that she is straddling a marlin spike upon which she gently moves up and down, up and down, swaying in the sea's swell, in all her beauty, there in the bows, singing a lilting song. Her red hair, her loose silken gown are flying in the wind. She smiles at him, sings "Come hither love to me." He luffs the sails and is about to step across into her boat when her song changes into inarticulate howls, and he sees she is swathed in torn bandages seeping pus, St Elmo's fire running up and down the scarecrow masts, illuminating the shape that was hers. He leaps back into his own craft and flies before the wind. He must steer with courage and hope. Any lapse in concentration will surely mean death by drowning. Darkness will ensnare him before he reaches that distant coast. He will be unable to see the reef that protects it, he will hear only the dull roar of the breakers. Behind him comes that ominous hull, ahead lies the coast. That coast is peopled by ruthless savages, and is called Wreck Coast; God help any sailor driven upon it. "Trust only in the permanence of sorrow," Fludd tells himself, as he runs before the gale.

The Fifth Car

the desert. A world of sand of many colours, parched by sun, assails him. Fludd searches in vain for shade. The plain teems with poisonous snakes, and, most deadly, scorpions scuttling amongst rocks. Somewhere in the midst of the wilderness a muddied waterhole surrounded by palm trees awaits him. The desert is littered with skeletons; some of the skulls are human. She rides towards him on an Arab stallion, the sun gleaming on her burnished brown hair, her long brown hair her only garment, her skin golden in the fading sun. She is smiling, offering him a drink from a leather bag. His heart is bursting with love. As she swings her leg over to

dismount, his heart soars at the glimpse of her pink sex. He raises
the leather bag to his mouth and pours ashes into his greedy
throat. Choking, he looks into the empty sockets of a skull, a
skeleton clattering to the sand in front of him, a rattlesnake rearing
at him out of the bones. Fludd flees once more, sensing all around
him the wraiths of savage Tuareg horsemen, waiting, waiting for the
darkness. "Joy is the shadow of earthly pain," Fludd tells himself, as
he flees.

The Sixth Car

the jungle. Fludd must hack a path with his machete through
barriers of bamboo. Clouds of mosquitoes blind him, killer-bees attack, army ants sting, bloodsuckers attach themselves lovingly to his
limbs as he wades through the green scum of the swamps. A boa
constrictor, like a great moving jigsaw puzzle, heaves on a branch
above his sweating head. Death-masks hang from creepers.
Shadows flit behind gross ferns, and he fears the prick of a blow-
dart. Fetid streams block his progress, brimming with the razor-
jaws of piranha fish. At dusk, the clamour of the jungle abruptly
ceases, and ominous silences chill him. She appears just before
dark, from behind the great lianas. Her hair is black, her naked
body oiled and perfect. She smiles reassuringly, and lies on the
jungle floor, opening her dark crotch to him. His love is boundless,
he discards his clothing and lies down beside her. As darkness
descends, he hears the inhuman laughter of the jungle, sees the
twin fangs protrude from red lips as she moves her mouth towards
his neck. Fludd does not recoil. He smiles, embraces her with great
affection. For the first time he thinks of no words, tells himself absolutely nothing.

The Seventh Car

the car of rest for the traveller. A cottage with spruce sides stands
on a meadow, green and misty, hills in the distance are luminous
with snow. Streams criss-cross the parkland in the cool light. From
the cottage, manicured lawns run to the edge of the deep woods
where fawns perform a quadrille. The walls of the main room of
the cottage are blue. A large four-poster bed and an armchair take
up the centre of the room. Blue curtains fringe the bed, the sheets

are fresh and blue. A servant girl dressed in white will escort the traveller to the bath, where she will wash him tenderly, massage his weary body with odorous oils. She will dry him and help him into light pyjamas. She will bring to his bedside a tray of delicacies so that he may assuage his hunger. She will collect the tray, draw the curtains and leave him to his dreamless sleep.

The Seventh Car awaits Ireneus Fludd and we await him outside the door of the Seventh Car. It is now three weeks since he set out on his journey through the Train of Gardens. Rescue parties have searched for him with fatal results. Only one survivor, torn and terribly injured, fought his way back to the entrance of the First Car and staggered out, gibbering. But as yet, no one has given up hope. Many of the friends of Fludd assemble each morning outside the Train, daily bulletins are given. Watonobe (she is very beautiful and very sad) has arrived from Oluba, and awaits, as we all await, the triumphal return of Ireneus Fludd.

The Hobby

The Hobby

The wrinkles on his face were as complex as a railroad junction, a chain of mandalas converging on his eyes and mouth. Somewhere within them lay a secret not disclosed by the facts: sixty years working for the LMS (London-Midland-Scottish), a terminal "thank-you-very-much," a silver pocket-watch in remembrance. Began his travels then, always by train, and came to be in Southern Ontario for a time, took a room with a Kitchener man and his wife who'd only ever boarded a cat before, never had a human being winter over with them.

Like a cat, too, he nuzzled around their house on the first day, unselfconscious, sniffing into all the corners, a lithe old man looking for a particular place. And settled on the basement. The man and his wife agreed to install a bed there. The basement was his. He brought down his suitcase, later his wooden box of equipment. He told them that between journeys he liked to build his own railroad, an old man's hobby, an old man with railroads on the brain. Who hoarded words like nuts, occasionally squandering them in reminiscences. As on a morning of snow in January:

"There was a lot of snow that day. Still the plough should have been able to clear the lines. They nearly had to cancel the parade.

That was a good fire in the waiting-room, but the station-master wouldn't let us enjoy it. 'Do this, do that.' Keeping the platforms clear for the spectators. We were just as glad when the trains arrived. They came right out of the snow. The Flying Scotsman, the Royal Scot, the Caerphilly Castle, the Lord Nelson, the Princess Elizabeth. You could see the names right on their sides. Those engineers ignored us as though we weren't even there waving and shouting at them. The noise made us forget the cold. The ground was trembling and people were laughing, even the station-master, and he never used to laugh. After they were all past he said, 'You'll not see anything like that again.' I said, 'Maybe not.' "

Always remembering the old days on the railroads. But talking was not his hobby, he had to get on with his work behind the locked basement door. Then he would emerge late in the day, grimy, nod over a snack, and off to bed. He always locked the basement door after him and made it plain they must on no account go down until he had finished his work, whenever that might be. For he had so much to do, laying the tracks, wiring the dynamos, installing complicated parallels, cycles, assembling the platforms, the station itself.

Yet by the end of January they suspected he was nearly finished, for one night as they sat in the living-room overhead, they heard what sounded like a train pecking its way along the tracks. They smiled and went to the basement door. But the noise stopped and he did not answer their knock.

Next day he told them they must be patient, he would not abide prying into his work. Right now he was organizing a full timetable and was too busy to amuse sightseers. He had crews to dispatch, mail-loading to supervise, tracks to inspect, all the burdens of assembling an intricate operation.

They co-operated. Instead of setting a place for him at table, they would leave his dinner on a tray at the door of the basement. Often when they went to pick up the tray they would find the meal untouched and so they worried about his health too. When he did consent to come to table, it was usually by way of celebration, some difficult piece of machinery successfully installed. He would wash the grease from his face and hands, and sit cheerfully, quietly, his mind elsewhere planning the next move. Only on Sundays would he luxuriate in bed late, storing up strength for the Monday-morning onslaught. On one of those Sundays, he rose late and had lunch with them. Over coffee he looked at them directly and spoke:

"That boy wore me out. I tried to get him to help me build a railroad after I retired. I showed him how to put it together and how to fix it when it broke down. But the tunnel frightened him the way it gobbled things down like a snake. I told him you couldn't do without a tunnel. He said he was scared it would swallow him, and me too, if I didn't look out. He just wanted to sit upstairs in his room, all alone, like he always did. She was the one that found him in the bath, and she never recovered from that. I always feel bad when I think about it, for I loved them both, and I think they loved me."

They wondered what he meant by it all, but he looked desolated, and they could think of nothing to say.

Mostly at table he listened absently to their small talk now, every so often checking his LMS silver pocket-watch with furrowed brow. They sensed that he grudged the time away from his hobby. When they would gently try to interest him in a stroll along the neat, tree-lined Kitchener streets, or coax him to come with them in the car to inspect the lush Mennonite farmlands of Waterloo County, or see Niagara Falls, he would excuse himself, pointing out, as to irresponsible children, that there were schedules that had to be met. For their part, they accepted all his rebukes with remorse, perhaps pride. They were thankful for him, their lives were curiously purposeful as they had seldom been before.

And now a manic period began. He would start work in the basement at first light and they would hear him hammering urgently all day long and into the night. Whenever they saw him he was covered in grease, eyes red-rimmed, clothes dirty. His face had become so wrinkled it might have been a mask under which a stranger hid. They fretted over his neglect of himself, they did not want him to die on them from exhaustion. Yet their concern seemed to menace him, and he would mutter cagily that they should not worry, he was used to this, his railroad must be finished on time.

They did not have long to wait.

The next Sunday morning. Two A.M. They had gone to bed at

midnight, he had stayed up late, working in the basement. A tremendous howl awakened them abruptly, the whole house vibrated with it. Oh my God, they thought as they rushed downstairs into a cloud of foul smoke that made them wheeze and cough, he's set the place on fire.

The basement door was locked from the inside. A terrifying grinding and screaming came from behind it. They stood helpless, then put their bodies resolutely to the door and splintered it open. They stumbled inside onto the landing at the top of the little staircase, and through the smoke they saw his work.

Under the dim ceiling lights, the basement was transformed. It was now a grimy old British railway station bustling with activity. On the platform beneath them a swarm of people they had never seen before, one of them carrying a baby in her arms, jostled onto a single passenger carriage attached to a huge, old-fashioned glistening black locomotive, a monster of hissing steam. A golden LMS was emblazoned on its side. Paralysed, they watched as officious-looking porters in dowdy uniforms with tin buttons began slamming the carriage doors behind the last passengers, and an amplified voice whined something about a departure. Other travellers on the congested platform seemed to have recently disembarked and uncertainly escorted trolley-loads of luggage pulled by brisk porters towards various murky apertures. A guard waved a red flag.

That was when they saw him. He was in the engineer's cabin, leaning his left elbow on the window ledge, peering ahead of the train up into a vast tunnel. The brakes exhaled numbingly. The wheels began slowly to lumber towards the tunnel. With his right arm they saw him reach expertly in front of him and pull back and forth, back and forth. A shattering double wail permeated the air. He glanced back in their direction for a moment. He was all concentration, he was all contentment.

They did not know what moved them. Hand in hand they rushed down the stairs in desperation, yanked open the last door of the moving carriage and scrambled aboard. One of the porters slammed the door shut behind them as the train entered the tunnel.

A sudden silence. The smell of stale cigarette smoke. Before them stretched an aisle giving access to half a dozen compartments.

As they swayed along the aisle, the passengers behind the glass paid no attention to them: some were reading newspapers, some conversing with their neighbours, some staring idly out of the windows into the darkness, the train advancing further into the tunnel picking up speed. All the compartments were filled except for the very last, marked "FIRST CLASS." The only occupant was a bushy-haired man who loured up at them as they gazed in. Distantly they heard the engine screech a muffled defiance of the darkness. They entered the compartment, slid the door shut and sat down opposite me. They told me how they came to be on that train. Then they asked me who I was, and we looked at each other with growing anxiety.

One Picture of Trotsky

One Picture of Trotsky

"The women's cloaks were as black as the morning," she said.

I'm sure that's what she said. Then again, maybe I heard wrong. She's been mumbling a lot and I can't make out much of it. Something about morning. She doesn't sleep much, she just lies here, dozing, on and off. Something about the morning being black and cold.

Start with a morning, black and cold, make the sun quick to withdraw its probing finger from an opening in the low horizon. Let there be women, thirteen of them, in hooded cloaks, standing in a huddle on the cobble-stones in front of the prison. They might have been a death-fleet, their black sails flattened by the gale that howled across miles of ocean and harrowed the coastal plain.

It was almost six o'clock. Behind the prison's massive granite walls, a drum rolled deeply. Then a sharper drumming: hobnailed boots rattling against stone, the boots of the death squad leading out the prisoner.

He seemed very relaxed, sitting there, legs crossed, on the stool by his crib. The chaplain asked him if he'd like to say a prayer or two, but he declined, politely. He said he wished the prison breakfasts had always been as good. He had treated the guards with great courtesy all the night before, and when he turned in, around midnight, he told them not to be afraid to wake him during the night if they needed an extra hand at cards. Naturally, they did not disturb him. The warden's message came at ten minutes to six: no reprieve. He showed no sign of disappointment. When he heard, a few minutes later, the sound of the escort coming along the corridor, he rose and smoothed his clothes. He thanked the chaplain for his company during the past days, and was sorry he couldn't oblige him in the matter of prayer. He shook hands with the guards, squeezing the shoulder of each of them affectionately. They seemed embarrassed when he told them they should be proud of the way they'd done their unpleasant duty. The escort arrived at the cell door, and he greeted them cheerfully. He allowed the officer to manacle his hands, then marched away at the head of the escort with a confident stride.

The women strained their ears. The boots and the drum had fallen silent, even the wind no longer whined. The stitching of minutes was nearly done.

A shout of command, the crash of a trapdoor. It was over. Now the wind could begin its whining again.

The women outside crowded around the oak prison door with its metal studs. They were all attention as the locks rasped, the door creaked ajar. It was the hangman, wearing half a face, half a mask, holding a lantern. One of the women curtsied, and he held his lantern high, looking her over, looking them all over through his slits. He signalled them to come into the prison-yard, one by one.

The yard was empty. They could see no one but the hangman's masked assistant, all of the soldiers and officials having hurried inside out of the cold. The assistant stood in the middle of the yard beside the scaffold, a wooden skeleton of ribs and props, filtering the light of torches. No one else. Though there may have been onlookers. From hundreds of barred windows around the yard, was there a blur of faces?

But the attention of the women focused on the gallows, their eyes yearned towards it. From the cross-beam of new wood, a body swung on a rope, to and fro, swaying gently in the wind, alive with flickering torchlight. The head tilted at an impossible angle in its black cover.

The hangman's slit eyes looked around the women.

"Which one?" he asked, his voice soft, high-pitched.

One of the women, taller than the others, stepped forwards. He reached a gloved hand out and slid her hood back to her shoulders. Her head was shaved, a young woman with jowels. She did not look him in the eyes.

By now, the hangman's assistant had lowered the rope so that the feet of the hanged man, like those of an idle puppet, lightly brushed the damp cobble-stones under the scaffold. The women ducked through the framework and began to undress the dead man. They did not bother with his upper clothing, for his hands were still cuffed behind him. They pulled his rough canvas trousers down round his black boots. His lower body was exposed to them all.

They looked to the bald woman. She did not waste time. She lifted her skirts above her heavy thighs and tucked them in. She put her arms round the dead man's neck and heaved herself up, strad-dling him, wrapping her legs around his buttocks, agile as a moun-tain climber. The rope creaked with the double burden. She began to bob up and down on him, straining in that cold dawn in the light of the torches. The hangman looked on, as did his assistant, and the twelve cloaked women, and perhaps another hundred pairs of eyes at a hundred barred windows.

The bald woman pumped up and down more and more quick-ly, sighing, grunting, a pennant of saliva flying from her open mouth. Then she stiffened, and whimpered loudly for a moment. She sighed, her body relaxed, and she slid to her knees on the cob-blestones, her arms still clinging to the dead man's legs, her face in his groin.

The hangman wasted no time. He took her by the arm and gent-ly raised her up. His small hands began untying the strings that kept the black bag on the dead man's head. He pulled the sack away. In the light of the torches, they saw the face of the hanged man, his smooth skin, his black hair wet, even in that cold morning wind, with the sweat of dying. He would have been a handsome man, except for his bulging eyes, but for his tongue, swollen and purple, protruding from between his lips. But for his neck. The rope had squeezed his neck so tightly, because of the double weight, it was the width of a thumb.

The hangman gave an order in his soft voice, and herded the women to the prison gate. He pulled back the big iron latch, leaning his shoulder against the gate till it creaked open wide enough to release the women into the blustery wind of the morning.

She's a loner, an old Scottish woman. She still has an accent, though she came here a long time ago. She's well liked, but she isn't sociable. She won't go to parties or anything like that. She's not a talker, you can't get anything out of her about her past. She was tall and heavy when I first met her, before the illness. She's slim now, deadly slim, so she says.

I could get a good angle-shot of her now, with the light coming in over her left side, making interesting shadows on the pillow.

She's mumbling again, years and places. Maybe something to do with her anthology. I don't know.

That would be in the winter of the year 1879, say, in a city on the north-east coast of Scotland. Let the cloaked women be members of The Pillars of Absalom, a cult formed in honour of the biblical King David's son, Absalom, who was hanged from a tree without leaving any children behind him. The women of the cult told everybody who would listen that one day a virgin would bear a child to a hanged man and the child would continue the line of Absalom, and, indeed, of David.

These Pillars of Absalom made their pilgrimage from prison to prison, from hanging to hanging (it was an age of hangings), occasionally finding a sympathetic or corrupt executioner. Men who were hanged, the women believed, achieved great erections and could reach orgasm even after death.

The name of the dead man, that dark dawn, is unknown. But the virgin was a woman of some education, Jenny Morrison, who had joined the cult just a few months before. She became pregnant in due course as a result of her union with the corpse. No one can say whether she was the only Pillar of Absalom to conceive in this way.

In November 1879, Jenny Morrison gave birth to twins, a boy and a girl.

At the time there was a rumour that the old midwife who saw the little boy and girl slide out of their mother's womb onto the gloomy bed thought they must be Siamese twins. Then she realized that in fact the babies were linked together in pre-natal incest, the boy's tiny erect penis jammed inside his sister's tiny vagina. According to the rumour, the midwife held them up by the ankles, and had to slap their tiny backsides over and over again before they separated with an unearthly howl.

That was the rumour. What is sure is that Jenny Morrison died of complications a week after the birth, and that her parents, who did not mourn their daughter's death, agreed to raise the twins as their own.

So Jenny Morrison died too early to meet Leon Trotsky. In fact, she died a few days before he was born. If they ever had met, she would certainly have asked him if his real name, Lev Davidovitch, meant he was by any chance a true descendant of King David. And, depending on his answer, she might have adored him.

Every now and then she says, "Trotsky," when she's dozing. I asked her once, when she was lucid, what's this about Trotsky? Do you mean the Russian revolutionary? I didn't know you were interested in politics. She said, "It was a long time ago, a long time ago." I told her Trotsky was dead now, I read that he was assassinated in Mexico a few weeks ago, did she know? She said, "I know."

She's dozing again. Poor Abigail. Mumbling about light or night, I can't tell which. Poor Abigail.

Gaslight is needed now, gaslight struggling with night in those streets, or hissing down angrily from the dark areas where the gas mantles are broken. Let it be Saturday night, wet and foggy. Saturday night was the night of fog, always, in the city.

The man was middle-aged, drunk. He would lurch to his left or his right, then steady himself till he gained confidence, then reach out with his right leg, his antenna for testing the spongy mattress of pavement. If he'd listened, he'd have heard the quiet steps behind him. Perhaps he did listen, stop, look back a moment, think he saw something. But didn't care. No, this man whooped a little instead, danced a brief jig, lost his balance again, then staggered on, singing loudly, "Sheee's the bonnieee laaass from Baaallochmyyyyle. ..."

He rolled on like this for a few more blocks, till his walk became a run, and he swung suddenly up a dark alley off the main street. By the back wall of a factory, he began fumbling at his fly, baring his teeth, shuffling in discomfort. His urine sprayed the wall noisily. He sighed, and began buttoning up again.

Did he not hear, at that moment, the soft voice that spoke his name? He should have turned around instead of beginning to hum good-naturedly, for then he might have avoided the thin blade that slid smoothly into his back, again and again, till he fell on his face in the puddle of his own water, thinking something inside of him had ruptured, thinking his body had betrayed him in some agonizing way, seeing only at the last, from the corner of his dying eyes, a figure bent over him in a long coat, an arm stabbing, stabbing, stabbing, feeling, at the moment of death, the blood seep from a dozen cracks in his broken body.

Her doctor says to try to keep her cheerful. But that's not necessary when she's awake. And when she starts sobbing in her sleep you can't very well wake her up just to tell her to cheer up. Maybe it's the pain gets to her sometimes, so she's entitled to weep in her sleep. I wouldn't tell her about it though, or she'd ask me to take a picture. I know it. She'd love to see a picture of it.

A link between the stabbings is needed. All committed, say, in the same slum district. Otherwise, they appear quite random. Men, women, and even a young boy who was out of doors too late died by the knife in those dark streets. Fear filled that city, where to be born in the first place seemed like punishment enough.

It turned out that the murderer was a local priest, widely known as a stern man. His housemaid reported him to the police one spring morning. She had become afraid because she had noticed blood on his clothing all winter. He himself showed no surprise when two detectives came to visit him, and he was quite willing to talk. He said he had, for years, listened in his confessional box to all the seedy sins, the same sins, repeated again and again. He had tried in vain to heal the sinners with the holy words. But they didn't want to be healed, only to hear the words.

So he turned to punishment. He could see plainly that the Church's authorized penances were not severe enough. He felt called to be a divine avenger, a butcher knife in the hand of God.

He began his mission of killing. He did not care who his victims were: one blood sacrifice was quite as good as another when all were guilty. For example, the night he killed the twelve-year-old boy, he had actually been on watch outside the house of a woman who was a recurrent sexual sinner. She had decided not to sin that night, it seemed. So he made up his mind to kill instead the boy with the innocent face who approached him in the shadows and asked, with a knowing look, if he needed anything tonight. No, there was no scarcity of sinners.

His trial was a sensation. The judge had to have him restrained, for he kept interrupting the proceedings, talking aloud to himself, his eyes staring ahead:

" 'I will destroy man whom I have created from the face of the earth...they shall all be put to death, being filled with all unrighteousness, fornication, wickedness, covetousness, maliciousness, full of envy, debate, deceit, malignity... Whisperers, backbiters, haters of God, despiteful, proud, boasters, inventors of evil things, disobedient to parents, covenant breakers, they which commit such things are worthy of death.' "

The officers of the court tried to silence him, but he began shouting, hysterical:

"I have done what he commanded: 'I shall slaughter them all like doves of the valleys each for his sin...let not your eye spare, neither have ye pity: old men, young men, virgins, children, women, kill and exterminate them all.' " Shouting in a huge voice, foam in the corners of his mouth, that he had done his duty.

Now he looked about him, realizing where he was, and he called down curses on the court, telling them they too were sinners, every one of them, and that they had no right whatever to sit in judgement on him, the messenger of God. That God hated not only sin, but sinners too, and that none of them would escape in the end.

"Heaven and earth shall pass away," he shouted, "but my words shall not pass away."

His own body crushed him to death. Three years later, that was, in
a prison for the criminally insane. One morning he had a seizure
in which the powerful muscles of his upper body, the pectoralis
major and minor, the deltoideus, latissimus dorsi, teres major and
trapezius combined and contracted with such force that they bent,
and then snapped his bones in half, his sternum, clavicle, scapula,
thoracic vertebrae and every rib in their reach. He roared in agony,
and thrashed about, but the orderly on duty could only stand and
watch the jagged edges of some of the broken bones burst out of
the flesh, while, at the same time, inside his ruined chest, the ragg-
ed ends of the ribs punctured his lungs, so that blood spouted from
his mouth and nostrils, a whale, sounding before plunging deep into an invisible sea.

   The name of the priest was the Reverend Ebenezer Morrison
(known as Ebby, when he was a boy), one of the Jenny Morrison
twins. His body crushed him in the year 1910. He was thirty years
old, the same age as Leon Trotsky. He had never heard of Trotsky,
but if he had, he would certainly have condemned him as just
another sinner, guilty as all the rest.

There she goes again, "Trotsky." As though he was an old friend. I
wonder if she had friends anyway, if she ever was in love, back in the
Old Country. Maybe that's what's going through her mind, lying in
this bed. One of her old lovers.

   She never used to say much about her life. The only things she
ever talked to me about were her work, or sometimes, her anthology. And even at that, not very much. She learnt photography
by herself. She's down to earth about it, no frills. Leave the thing
alone, she'd say, it's the thing that makes the picture, not the
photographer.

   There she goes again. I think it's her own name she's saying now,
over and over. Yes, that's it. Abigail, Abigail.

Abigail at last. Abigail Morrison in her hospital bed under a red
blanket in a linoleum-floored private ward. Every morning she
turns her face towards the window, waiting for the dawn, for the bit-
ter lips of the horizon to spit the sun back into the world.

Yet she breathes more easily this morning, she does not at this moment feel (though this may be a bad sign) the disease creeping through her internal organs. She has noted how it infiltrates, digs in for a while, takes over the territory piece by piece. It has been hiding inside her all these years, waiting. She admires its patience, knows it will wait a little longer still, till she is ready to die.

Abigail Morrison remembers the past. Every night, every day when the nurses and doctors will leave her in peace, she remembers. Though by now she wonders whether it is indeed the past she remembers, or her most recent version of it.

She would swear to this: her family was cursed, she herself saved by a miracle. To be fathered by a corpse. To be the daughter of such a mother. To be the sister of a murderer, her brother. Ah! Ebby. Her playmate, long ago. The love in him cut down, till only the stubble, the harsh prickles were left. She cannot think about him any more, it frightens her so much.

Abigail looked like her mother, they said, tall and heavy. But she loved everything alive. She was in her early thirties when she met Daniel, in his worn suit, a frail man who played the violin, a man with kind blue eyes, and she went to live with him. She loved him so much for loving her, she could hardly bear to look in his blue eyes.

At his cottage on the outskirts of the city, Daniel gave her a gift of a box camera, and showed her how to look at things and take pictures of them. She began to see everything for the first time: a thistle in rain, a hare limping in a field, a wall stone-grey in the morning, the dark green of the potato fields. Everything was charged with beauty.

Daniel was the subject of her first photographs, sitting with his violin in light or shadow, his dog beside him, still suspicious of the newcomer with the clicking box. She took so many pictures of Daniel in his every mood that, after a while, he became quite unselfconscious. Even the dog, in time, would admit to the camera's click only by the slightest flick of an ear.

For brief periods Abigail knew she was beautiful. Some days they would not leave the house, but spend the whole day naked. They would love each other's bodies, fondling and manipulating, rubbing against each other. They loved to inarticulateness. For hours on end their only conversation would be:

"Abigail."

"Daniel."

Again and again.

Yet sometimes when he was lying on her, exhausted, she thought that together they were a kind of sarcophagus, she was the squat tomb underneath, he was the carved miniature of a dead man. Her earlier pictures only impressed on Abigail how he was fading. In them, he was more substantial, more real than he was now in the flesh.

Daniel caught pneumonia that first autumn (they had lived together for only three months), shivering on the cold bus back from giving one of his lessons, and began, without delay, to wheeze his life away. She put him to bed. She hugged him, naked, warming him with her own naked body. It had always worked before, but this time he could not stop dying. He only kept muttering that he had to finish learning the piece he'd been working on for the last few weeks. She knew he couldn't bear to die till he'd mastered it. He wanted the violin always on his bedside table, and he would reach for it and play feebly from time to time.

She took pictures of her dying Daniel: every moment he had left was a gift to her. One day, around noon, he came out of a shallow sleep, sat up and reached for the violin. With trembling fingers he began bowing, the sound grating on her ears. The dog was sitting up too, watching him with great concentration. She wanted to take the violin away from Daniel as he sat there shaking with fever, she wanted to stop him. She knew he was hearing something else.

He stopped at last, looked at her intently, then breathed:

"That's it."

He fell back on the pillow, the violin clanged to the floor. The dog barked, a hoarse bark she had never heard before.

She went to Daniel. She saw his eyes glazed now beyond sickness.

"Abigail," he whispered, and died.

He was gone, and she was alone, a sad, heavy woman in an empty cottage. He once told her that amongst primitive men up the Amazon a father would pass on one of his lice to his child. They would laugh over that. She knew he would not have wanted his body to rot in a coffin. She paid a fisherman to row her out to sea

with the ashes of Daniel and his violin. A mile out in the firth, on
an overcast day, she sprinkled them into the green water and watched them slowly sink. She liked now to think of the fish nosing at
his remains. And sometimes she liked to think of herself down
there with Daniel in that clear water, each of them draped in ten-
drils of seaweed, making slow and rhythmic love.

So she had no one now. Her grandparents would not even come
to Daniel's funeral. She decided to make her move. She sold the
cottage which she could no longer bear to live in, and booked her
passage for Canada. She took with her only one small carrier bag,
and her camera.

She's weeping again. Her face is soaked in tears. I suppose I could
take a picture of her now, but I don't have her determination.

When it comes to taking pictures, she's not a shy woman at all.
Don't hesitate, she always tells me. As soon as it dawns on you, take
a picture of it. Good pictures are all around you.

She likes everything to be in pictures. She doesn't have any faith
in words.

Wartime, the spring of 1917. Let her board ship for Halifax, Nova
Scotia via New York on a Cunarder. Let it be an adventureless
voyage to New York, she, camera in hand wandering around the
great throbbing machine, prowling the glassed-in decks trying to
find the sea air. But, taking pictures of everything, for everything
was alive and new, and she could still hardly believe she was on a
ship in the middle of the Atlantic Ocean.

On the morning of March 26, in New York harbour — she was
now thirty-seven years old — she transferred to the Norwegian ship
Christianafjord, which was to call in at Halifax and disembark those
bound for Canada, then continue on its way to Norway. At noon
the ship cast off and ploughed along the sound, east past Cape
Cod, and north along New England, its foggy shore lurking in the
distance. Abigail spent as much of her time as possible on deck,
taking pictures of the dim coastline, hoping to give body to the
ghost.

The ship was quiet that voyage, for no one felt safe at sea in wartime, even on passenger ships. Abigail noticed that one family

would come up on deck each day and stand silently by the railing, bundled up in worn-looking clothes against the brisk spring winds. A man, a woman, and two boys of around ten. They would stare west, too, at the land, trying to will it visible, or they would move to the starboard side to watch the passing of small icebergs on the ocean's horizon.

The man was thin, taller than average, with sharp eyes behind oyster-shell glasses. Often he'd glance towards Abigail as she walked past with her camera, as though he would like to speak to her. Or he'd turn and say something quietly to his family in a foreign language. But he'd always nod to her politely. She would say hello, then shrink away, thinking how she must look to them, a big, ugly woman.

Sometimes she'd hear him at night at the dining-room table. He was a different man then, arguing aggressively with some of the ship's officers who would come over and sit with him. His wife and children would eat up their desserts then leave for their cabin after much kissing and hugging.

One of the passengers at her table told Abigail that the man was Trotsky, the revolutionary.

After a smooth voyage, the ship arrived at Halifax harbour. It was the third of April, another grey morning, only some swooping gulls and a few passengers like herself ready to disembark. But the ship had hardly docked when half-a-dozen naval policemen came up the gangway. Minutes later, they were dragging Trotsky by the arms along the companion-way to the deck, and down the gangway. He was shouting, but she couldn't make out what he was saying. The few passengers on deck, and the crew, watched. His wife and the two little boys stood looking down from the rail, saying nothing, doing nothing.

He eventually gave up struggling with the police and walked down the last few feet of the gangway.

When he stepped onto the dock, he hesitated. He looked back up to the deck where his family stood. Then he shouted something to them in that alien language, and the boys smiled happily back to him and waved. His eyes swept over the rest of the watchers on deck and caught Abigail's. He stared at her. She raised her camera and centred him in the viewfinder, still staring up at her. Snap! Then he was gone in a knot of uniforms.

So Abigail had a picture of Trotsky. He had not intended to stay in Canada at all, he was just passing, on his way back to Russia. Instead, he had to resign himself to twenty-six days in a Nova Scotia prison camp. At that time, his name meant nothing whatever to Abigail Morrison, but afterwards she heard it often. Whenever anyone spoke of his atrocities, which were frequently recorded in the newspapers, she would always say, "No. Not Trotsky. I have a photograph of him and I don't believe a word of it." He was the second man she had ever photographed.

Her eyes are twitching. She's smiling up at me. Abigail, you go right on sleeping, I'll be here for ages yet. Her lips are moving but I can't make out what she's saying. Her eyes are closing again.

Poor Abigail. Her hair's falling out, and the skin around her face has all caved in. Slim, all right. She'd be a stern-looking woman if it wasn't for her eyes. I wonder how they'd show up in a picture, they're so grey. She says looking through a camera often enough affects your eyes. You never see things again the way you used to.

Make the picture of Trotsky twenty-three years before. Let photography become her profession. She will settle in Toronto, and buy a new camera with tripod and accessories. She made a living taking photographs of newborn babies right in their homes, or in hospitals.

In the teaching hospital, a pathologist who had watched her with curiosity wondered if she'd be willing to photograph some dissections he was performing.

He took her down to his lab and showed her his work, observing her reactions, while he described the cases, gauging her nerve.

On the broad marble tables in the lab, two subjects lay under the cold lights, one of them covered by a sheet. Abigail Morrison at first thought the uncovered subject was a statue moulded in black, pitted metal. But trickles of red ooze were leaking from some of the pits. The left arm was half-severed by a metal saw whose teeth were clogged with flesh.

It was the body of a worker at the steel-mill who had fallen, just the day before, through the safety barrier and into a vat of molten ore. His workmates had looked on as he swam a few desperate strokes, screaming. He actually touched the side of the vat with his hand before he died. They scooped him out with the ladle, and as soon as the air hit the body, the metal began to solidify. The thing that the ambulance brought to the hospital was not a man, more a grisly work of art.

Normally, they'd just have buried him. But the pathologist wanted to see the effects of such a trauma. He suspected that the metal suit had become an elaborate can containing a thick meat stew. The body had been refrigerated overnight to keep it solid.

Abigail listened with interest to the pathologist's explanation of the case. She noted how the fragments of the man's clothing that remained and his boots had become ferrous, how the eyes were now steel ball-bearings, the penis a steel rod. How the body was still in the posture of a swimmer.

She said she would like to take some trial pictures, using the existing lighting in the lab, with the addition of one or two portable lights of her own.

The pathologist noted this response, then took her to the other table, and pulled back the sheet.

On the table lay a female, about twenty years old, already partially dissected. While she was alive, she had been unable to bear the sight of printed words. She claimed that the words rose from the page to attack her body like insects, or microbes, or, ultimately, like a plague.

During the early years of her life, her parents had humoured her, though they could see no marks on her body. They kept books and newspapers out of the house. And that seemed to work. But as she got older, there was no placating her. A newspaper in the pocket of a passer-by, an advert on the side of a trolley-car, would cause her to howl in pain.

Her parents took her to the best psychiatrists, but no one could talk her out of her disease.

In the last year of her life, nothing could stop the onslaught. She said she could see words everywhere in the air, flying at her from every library and bookseller's in the city, like mosquitoes, she said, scenting her out. She said they were now flying directly into her lungs, choking her. She could feel herself begin to rot on the inside.

The other morning, her parents found her dead.

Abigail could see no sores on the body, but a section of lung lying on the table was ripe with pustules.

She asked questions about incisions and amputations, and tested various angles for lighting to take the clearest pictures. The pathologist hired her.

After that, the police and the insurance companies asked regularly for her services. Hospitals employed her to photograph techniques used in the performance of tricky operations. Her pictures illustrated textbooks on anatomy and surgical procedures, *The Art of Dissection*, say, or *Scalpel and Surgeon*, and *An Encyclopedia of Disease, Common and Uncommon*. Everyone relied upon her discretion, upon the strength of her stomach.

But it was only in the last few years she had the idea for a book of her own. She had begun her professional career taking photographs of the newly born. Now she wanted to take pictures of people near to death, and make an album of them — an anthology of the dying.

Her undertaking was not an easy one. The regular hospitals would not grant her free range. So she went to the mental institutions, the old age refuges, the doss-houses off Yonge Street, anywhere she was allowed entry with her camera. She took pictures of old people, tears of grief on tired cheeks, or faces twisted in bitterness. Or eyes dull, careless, relieved perhaps that it would soon be over. She took pictures of the young, frightened, protesting against the verdict. Some of the children were unmoved, good as dead already. She recorded them all without discrimination.

She had a nose for the moment of death, she could sense it. She felt at times she was the keeper of a vulture which sat on its tripod at the bedside with patient, ruthless eye. It was her own eye, too.

Yet the dying were not hostile to her. She paid attention to them, valued their unique dances with death. Many of them, rather than asking for the consolations of religion, would send for her at the end. Her camera was, for them, an angel in a black cowl, but no longer frightening.

"Take it now," some would whisper, their last gesture in life. "Take it now."

I've seen the anthology. It looks like an ordinary family album in a loose binder. The first picture's old, taken in the 1880s perhaps, with a soft lens on dry plate and a silver halide emulsion in gelatin. It's a picture of a thick-set young woman with jowels. Her hair's swept back in a bun. She's wearing a high-necked blouse with a brooch in the collar, and a long skirt. She's the image of Abigail.

The second picture looks as though it's from the twenties. The lighting's a mix of magnesium powder and potassium chlorate. The picture itself is of a sharp-featured clergyman with his hair slicked back. His lips are full, but his eyes are cold.

Now come the pictures of the dying. The first one must have been taken by a box camera a long time ago on celluloid film with silver bromide emulsion. The angle is the same as in most of the others, from the left side of the subject at a height of about five feet.

The picture shows a sick man who seems quite young, lying in an old brass bedstead, lighted by a window. On the table beside the bed, there's a violin and a bow. The man's left hand is stroking the head of a black dog that hasn't come out well, only the nose and eyes. The man looks really sick, but he's got a smile for the one who took the picture.

Hundreds of pictures of dying people follow. They've all been taken more recently. Technically, they're like all Abigail's work. The lighting is muted, even when she's used the old gas-discharge flash tubes. They're not fancy, just straightforward, well-taken pictures.

"All you have to do is put the frame around them," she used to tell me. "Works of art are right there under your nose."

I must admit, I found it harrowing to look at the pictures of all those dying people.

The final page of the anthology took me by surprise. There's another old picture, and it isn't of somebody dying. It's been taken with a box camera from the railing of a ship. On the dock, a crowd of stevedores in workmen's cloth caps is watching a group of men in military uniforms. They're all gathered round a man in a long black coat. He doesn't have a hat on. His face isn't well defined, the lens is too weak for that, and the man's face too far away. He's bearded, and I think he's wearing glasses, glinting in the light. Of all the people down on the dock, he's the only one looking up at the camera.

He went indoors out of the warm Mexican sun reluctantly, for he had been enjoying his garden. His visitor was not a man he trusted or liked. They went upstairs to his study, and he sat down and brought the manuscript out of the desk drawer. The visitor stood behind him, asking nervously for his opinion of it. He cleared his throat to reply. The ice-axe struck him in the back of the head. He screamed, a thin scream, but managed to get to his feet, pushing the chair aside. Everything was clear. He hugged his assailant to him, carrying both bodies to the floor. The scream had brought his wife and his bodyguards running upstairs to the study. When he saw them, he rose from the floor and staggered towards them, the axe still wedged in his skull. His wife whimpered, took him in her arms and gently lowered him to the floor. He knew that the substance dripping from his head onto the polished wood was a mixture of blood and brain.

Beside the picture on the final page of the anthology, there's a space for one last picture. Funny how, with just the outlines, it looks like the blueprint of a grave. It's where Abigail wants me to put her own last picture, unidentified, like all the others. She wants me to take it at the very last minute.

I made all the arrangements at her bedside. I rigged a flash camera with a magnifying lens on an intravenous pole. While I was doing it, she watched me like a scientist at the crucial stage of an experiment.

Let her compose an epilogue to her anthology. Let her have a voice. "None of us are dead. These photographs have no past tenses, no adjectives or adverbs, no subjunctives. They ask and answer no questions, fight no revolutions. They destroy nothing, except time."

She's mumbling again. "Time," I thought she said. And that sounded like "revolution." I suppose she's thinking about Trotsky. She'll be as dead as he is soon enough. I try to stay at her bedside as long as I can, but she's afraid I'll leave, for a coffee, or for forty winks. She made me fix the camera up with a delayed action shutter. She says if I'm not here when she's ready to die, she'll just have to get out of bed, press the shutter, and that'll give her twelve seconds to get back in bed. She'll see the flash and hear the click. Then she'll die in peace. I'm to develop the film with care, the way she taught me, then fix it to the space on the final page of her titleless anthology. She says there's nothing to it.

Lusawort's Meditation

Lusawort's Meditation

It is noon.

John Julius Lusawort's body is in the supine position. Abed. Yet the world continues to flaunt itself before his open eyes. Through the bedroom windows, for example, these things divert him: a church steeple threatening to puncture the scudding November clouds, a factory chimney spouting its tubers of black smoke, the tops of maple trees jigging erratically at the corner of the frame. Nearer hand, other prodigies thrust themselves forward: the chiaroscuro of rumpled sheets and blankets, the charcoal hair and heavy sprawl of the woman Fatima beside him, the hulks of chairs and dresser crowding the bed. Yes, the world bombards him. He is, as always, unwilling to resist. Nonetheless, Lusawort summons all his will-power, forces himself to think on the fate of da Costa, the bow-legged Azorean.

Da Costa was formerly Lusawort's friend. Da Costa the Azorean harpoon-master. On frosty winter evenings in Ontario he would recall for Lusawort those days of his youth in the ocean-fringed Azores, how the men of the Azores hunted, in their flimsy row-boats, the great whales. Through the bright air, the boats would creak away from the wooden dock, planks wet with dew, red-tiled, white-walled houses slipping aft, volcanic shores sheering off. The boats would slide across the azure water that met, somewhere, the azure sky, towards the distant gleam of the black blisters of whales.

Smoothly rowing, they would laugh over morning rolls and red wine, till gradually the blisters swelled into sea-monsters. Now there would be tension in the air. Da Costa would stand up in the bow, balancing himself against the motion, weighing the harpoon above his right shoulder, alert for the strike.

"Seem, I had a gift, Hohn Hulius," he confessed once, not boasting. (This "seem" that introduced his statements, like a hook for reeling in the words, Lusawort at first took to be a sign of da Costa's diffidence. It was, in fact, the Portuguese *sim* for "yes.")

"Seem, sometimes the whales knew my harpoon and dived deeply before I could get to them."

But whales from other reaches of the ocean, not recognizing da Costa, would linger too long and he would impale them unerringly.

He remembered the time the big bull whale challenged his arm. Da Costa struck, but still it foamed in on them and smashed boat after boat. It tried to find da Costa in the crimson water, spurning the others, singling him out. But the harpoon had done its job, and at last the bull plunged away, howling.

Long, grizzled John Julius lies abed, immersed in memories of stumpy, bow-legged Captain Ahab da Costa.

Time passed, whales dwindled in number, stayed away from the islands. Da Costa made preparations to come to the New World for other work. He told Lusawort about his farewell party and how the whole island came, the men in their Sunday suits, dead drunk. Da Costa remembered best what was said by the priest who, alone perhaps, was sober.

"Seem, he told me not many men were best in the world at a thing. He told me I was best in the world with the harpoon. Seem, the whales avoid the islands because of me."

Da Costa laughed sadly as he remembered this. Lusawort could see that the memory of greatness had failed to console him.

Many such things he told Lusawort to while away winter evenings. But after a year working for the Ford Motor Company, da Costa seemed to lose interest in his memories. Now when he spoke it was about his fears. He remarked casually one day that objects were try-ing to penetrate his body. Everything he saw, for example, seemed to enter through his eyes and bite into his brain. He could not understand why this should be so, but he must protect himself. He kept his eyes lidded as much as he could and wore dark glasses to blunt the sharpness of the images:

"Seem, Hohn Hulius, the light harpoons my eyes."

Lusawort, sensing da Costa's anxiety, congratulated him on his circumspectness.

Soon da Costa was trying to defend himself against the torment of sound. He began to wear ear-plugs as well as his dark glasses:

"Seem, you must understand, Hohn Hulius," (this in the loud voice of the deaf), "the noise attacks me."

In reply, Lusawort roared his approval of this defensive measure.

Da Costa quit his job with the Ford Motor Company. Lusawort wondered how he would live, how he would eat. This turned out to be a minor problem, for even food began to offend da Costa. He could hardly bear to eat and drink and tried to convince Lusawort to abstain with him:

"Seem, Hohn Hulius, it is foolish to permit bad things to enter at the mouth."

He was never more content than when defecating or urinating the intruders out of himself.

Smells finished him off.

Lusawort remembers how da Costa, sitting now at a safe distance, in dark glasses, ears plugged, shouted this confession:

"Seem, the smells, Hohn Hulius! The smells are too hard for me!"

He would occasionally wear a gauze face-mask but found the intimate contact with his own breath intolerable. The smells were insidious. Of differing intensities and densities, they moved at ground level the way clouds do in the upper air. Da Costa would navigate amongst them in constant peril. Often, seemingly clear passages became exitless fjords.

John Julius Lusawort thinks of da Costa at bay, unable to escape the treachery of the smells that clung to his clothing, his hair, waiting for a chance to infiltrate the orifices of his body.

Da Costa's own last act of penetration, to the certain knowledge of Lusawort, was into the body of this same fleshy Fatima, stirring now luxuriously in the bed beside him. Lusawort, all affection, kneads her plump breast and she giggles in her sleep. Da Costa had bequeathed her to him (how could a friend refuse?), for he had come to loathe the sight, touch, taste, and — oh! — the smell of her:
      "Seem, Hohn Hulius, she has the smell of island goat."
      With impeccable logic, da Costa at last refused to allow the tainted air to enter his lungs. A week ago, in the quiet of Lusawort's room, he had held his breath till his heart stopped.

John Julius Lusawort meditates, therefore, upon his *late* friend, da Costa, the only man he has known, or is ever likely to know, who has been the best in the world at something. He wonders if da Costa was not, perhaps, too good to live. Unlike himself. For John Julius Lusawort considers he is not too good; hence, he eats too much, drinks too much, enjoys penetration. He sighs, without remorse, brushes his hip lightly against the succulent body of the adaptable Fatima. Ever receptive, he permits the sight of her brown flesh to assail his reverent eyes. He feels all his senses tingle. His meditation on death is over.

Anyhow in a Corner

Anyhow in a Corner

IS IT TRUE THAT YOU ARE A LOVER OF *OBJETS D'ART*?
His basement apartment does not please the eye. It is littered with
crumpled Donut House coffee cups, an assortment of empty li-
quor bottles, and hamburger boxes like beached oyster shells.
There are old newspapers a foot deep on the floor. From time to
time he will read one, a paragraph here and there — he has a mind
only for fragments — the *Globe* with his coffee, the *Sun* at his daily
squat. The others are utilitarian and free: sales-flyers together with
virgin bundles of university *Gazettes*. They are adequate to insulate
a poor man's coat, serviceable as dog-litter (his dog is asleep, bristling in dreams). The man is grey, not well preserved. He perches
on a wooden chair at a wooden table lit by a bare ceiling-light. Pen
and paper lie before him, but he is busy, thinking.

WHAT WOULD YOU DO IF YOU WON THE LOTTERY?
He thinks, if only someone, a patron, would supply his needs, he
would live like Sir Walter Scott, his idol, long dead. He would find
a River Tweed. Cold. Perhaps with trout in it, and a chill northern
ocean for its destination. He would require some hills, yes, for his
Eildons and Cheviots. He would insist on ruins (absolutely
essential), for he could not do without moonlight on Melrose Ab-
bey, or the black ruins of Dryburgh under a lowering Border sky.

DO YOU EVER THINK OF MOVING TO A MORE DESIRABLE RESIDENCE?

This man abhors imitation. Yet he would not hesitate to imitate Sir Walter. There must be, somewhere, an architect capable of building him a replica of Abbotsford on the curve of that cold river. He has no doubts about the structure (*she would have laughed, she would have called it, properly, his castle*), no doubts at all. It must assert its symmetry amidst an anarchy of trees, what with its turrets, moats, battlements, serried chimneys, barred windows, barbicans, portcullises, machicolation, with its newels and its quoins, and its colonnades, and its pilasters, and its acroteria, and its almighty megaron. Its pantiles and its spires. It must be, and this is foremost, a magnificent dog-kennel. His three dogs (let there be three) will have the run of its resplendent galleries, will mark out their territories against its Louis Quatorze furniture, and its baroque columns.

OUTLINE YOUR IDEA OF THE GOOD LIFE FOR US PLEASE.

Your library-cum-study is all you ever dreamed of, lined with worn, leather-bound volumes, the outer wall of glass, French windows opening onto verdant lawns and the aspen-lined river. You sit in a comfortable leather chair at a desk of carved oak, or lower your weary limbs into the underbelly of a massive couch. You warm your nether parts, when necessary, at the cavern of a fireplace, for you will have a fire blazing winter and summer. Your dogs sprawl on the shag carpet, scratching themselves luxuriously.

DO YOU LIKE THE IDEA OF A WRITER'S BEING SUPPORTED BY A PATRON?

Your patron's motives will, of course, be quite mercenary. As they should be. You will be acquired as though you were a penny black, or a silver Victorian spittoon. Or a likely-looking thoroughbred for the stable at the downs. Or another crew-member for the vast, ghostly, rarely used yacht. The patron will never actually read any of your books. But occasionally he will inquire if everything is all right, how things are working out. He tells you it will improve the image of his corporations to support the arts.

DESCRIBE YOURSELF IN A NUTSHELL TO OUR READERS.
Occupation: kept writer. Age: septuagenarian. Height: exiguous.
Build: oblate. Weight: diurnal fluctuations. Health: dyspnoeic.
Education: catalectic. Hobby: multibibe. Marital Status: …(*she died
too young she died too young she died too young she died*).

WOULD YOU SELECT A SHORT PASSAGE FROM YOUR
WORK FOR THE BENEFIT OF THOSE OF OUR READERS
WHO HAVEN'T TIME FOR READING?
When I was twenty-seven, ladies and gentlemen, I published
privately a book that caused a stir. I introduced some new
characters into an old plot, as follows:

> The *Nellie*, a cruising yawl, swung at her anchor without a flut-
> ter of sails, and was at rest. The flood had made, the wind was
> nearly calm, and being bound down the river, the only thing
> for it was to come to and wait for the turn of the tide.
>
> The sea reach of the Thames stretched before us like the
> beginning of an interminable waterway. Marlow sat cross-
> legged right aft, leaning against the mizzen mast. He had
> sunken cheeks, a yellow complexion, a straight back, an
> ascetic aspect, and, with his arms dropped, the palms of hands
> outwards, resembled an idol.
>
> Two strangers had signed on for our crew on that
> memorable sail. Let us call them the Actors, the small and the
> large. All day they had been stricken with that malaise
> peculiar to the sea (though as yet we had not left the river)
> which terrifies even the brave; now they were able, at last, with
> the dropping of the mainsail, to ascend the murky
> companion-way out of that dim interior, and noisily to usurp
> the placid deck, where Marlow sat, about to ruminate upon
> one of his inconclusive experiences. His reproving glare did
> nothing to silence the relieved babble of the Actors, freed
> from their involuntary imprisonment, like twin Lazaruses
> risen again from the womb of earth. Their names were Stan
> Laurel and Ollie Hardy.

That was how it began.

DO YOU HAVE TO REPORT REGULARLY TO YOUR PATRON OR WHAT?

You are, obviously, under some…obligations. Once in a while, the patron, as is only human, likes to display his collection. You receive your summons to the city. Even after all these years, it still excites you. *(How she would have loved these command performances.)* The patron's mansion, quite naturally, dwarfs Abbotsford. The guests usually number five hundred. On very special occasions, when you have, say, just finished a novel, he also invites several international reviewers (it would be unthinkable to refuse one of his invitations) to come a few days earlier and read it over. He's a businessman, and likes to know how his investment is doing. You are expected to read selections for the assembled guests. You follow Pablo Casals, precede Maria Callas. You are sandwiched between the principal dancers of the New York Ballet and the touring exhibition of the Picasso drawings. You must do your part. You are his writer. He has freed you from all the pressures that drag others down. He requires three copies of each of your works from his publisher, then orders the plates to be broken. You are not upset by this, not a bit. For you, it's the writing that counts. Getting it down on paper. Off your chest. What happens then is of no interest to you.

TELL US MORE ABOUT THIS ATTRACTION TO THE LONG DEAD SIR WALTER SCOTT.

I admire, ladies and gentlemen, Sir Walter, for many things, but mainly for his indifference to the fate of his writing. He would not admit — can you imagine? — that he was author of the Waverley novels. He would not discuss them with critics, or reviewers. He never read over galleys ("an old dog sniffing its own vomit"). He had done his part, the writer's part. He told the editors to do whatever they felt was necessary to make the things sell. He didn't care much about plots. He often forgot how a story began by the time he finished it. He wanted only to rush back to Abbotsford and his dogs.

THEY SAY YOU TAKE THE OCCASIONAL DRINK. ANY TRUTH TO IT?

You couldn't do without a manservant in a place like Abbotsford. A kind of valet. A retired boxer, let's say, with irreversibly deviated septum. To keep the autograph seekers and the media spies away. To replenish the glass. Yes, replenish the glass. To deliver you from the gins and oranges of outrageous fortune. To deliver you especially from white wine: androgynous filth for fairies. Scotch whisky is what you require. How much have you swigged of it in the last forty years?

$$
\begin{aligned}
& 26 \text{ ounces per diem} \\
& \text{for } 365 \text{ days} \\
=\ & 9490 \text{ ounces per annum} \\
& \text{for } 40 \text{ years} \\
=\ & 379600 \text{ ounces}
\end{aligned}
$$

Every one of them the best. How would you survive otherwise when you have your bad dreams?

WHAT KIND OF THING ARE YOU WRITING THESE DAYS?
He is moved by his own words as he never was before. For months (or is it years now?) he has laboured over one paragraph. Every time he rereads it, rewrites it, it halts him in his tracks. There is no going beyond it.

And I said to him, and he said to me, and I said to him, and he said to me, and I said and I said and I said, and he and he and he, and then and then and then, I said to him no and he said I agree and I said to him no and he said yes I agree, and I said said said, and he said said said, and then and then and then and then, and only then.

He has written innumerable combinations of it. Is it the long-awaited, long-feared summary of all he ever has written, ever will write? The diamond in the rubbish-heap? *(Would she have liked it?)*

DO YOU, LIKE EVERYONE ELSE, GET DOWN ON YOURSELF OCCASIONALLY?
At times he drinks more than usual, for on certain days everything is pitch black. He could even begin to envy the others their successes. It is a mood that comes on him for no good reason, like a

cold out of season. Against his will, he lifts the cover, sees the real thing. His life, like all the others, futile. Yet he does not, any more, resist as he once did. Is he too weak now, or too wise? These unwanted glimpses may be the only authentic part of his life. They are, at least, his own: his visions, unearned gifts, not to be rejected. He has learnt, armed with a twenty-six-ouncer, to accept their visitations. He has always emerged from them in due course. It seems entirely possible to him, nevertheless, that one day he will not emerge.

WHAT KIND OF READERS DO YOU HAVE IN MIND?

(There was a time, ladies and gentlemen, when I tried to please someone with my writing. But she's dead now, she's dead. I have never cared much about anyone else's opinion of my work. When I write, though, I still think, "Now would she enjoy this part?" or, "I'll leave this part in for her." That's what goes on in my mind. I write for the dead. There it is: my ideal audience is dead.)

TELL US ABOUT YOUR MOST MEMORABLE MOMENTS?

He sits at his desk, writing, perhaps rewriting. The tip of his pen slithers across the yellow notepaper, stutters, lashes out, poises itself for another wriggling advance. His sparse hair is lank and his bald-spot glistens, a pink balloon contained by a lattice of silver thread. Often his eyes become vacant, meditative, his writing slow and meditative. It is a habit of his to call his dog to him from where it lies on its bed of newspapers. Good-natured, it stretches, wags a stump of tail, sidles over to him, tongue lolling, positions its sleek head under his dangling hand. He pets it, caresses the soft ears automatically. After a few moments the hand stops its fondling and the dog sinks to the floor, sighs, resumes its slumber. The pen, with renewed vigour, weaves across the yellow paper.

AND YOUR LEAST MEMORABLE?

Some evenings, he writes nothing, he stares at nothing. Once in a while, he twitches. The dog's black ears prick, but there is no summons. Dog and man continue their comfortless meditations.

WHAT DO YOU MOST REGRET IN LIFE?

He is saddened by the knowledge that he will never again be loved. His body has buckled, bottom-heavy. There is no spring any more

in his steps. He still has all the parts, but they no longer work efficiently. The skin of his hands is flaky and blotched, the strong
hands inherited from generations of working men, now
tremulous, effete as a fairy's. The once-blue eyes are now yellowed,
lustreless as fried eggs. He is a victim of dispepsia, lumbago, and,
hardest to accept, piles. He would be afraid to sleep with a woman
(if he got any offers) for fear of what his body might and might not
do: the farts, the burps, the incautious snores, the humiliation of
impotence. *(Ah! but she could have told them how he once was. How each
had adored the other's fine, firm body. He is too fond now of his solitude. He
has neglected himself, in spite of all her warnings.)*

IS THAT AN OLD GIRLFRIEND YOU KEEP REFERRING TO OR WHAT?

*(Tell me did you ever see so fair a creature in your town before? Sweet lovely
mild. I kiss her eyes goodly as sapphires shining bright. I kiss her ivory-white
forehead. I kiss both her cheeks sun-reddened as apples. I kiss her lips tempting as cherries. I kiss her neck snowy as a marble tower. I kiss her breasts
luscious as bowls of cream. I kiss her belly smooth as alabaster. Where now
my lips are set my seal shall be. Lead me in my mine of precious stones. Lead
me in. To enter in these bonds is to be free.)*

WHAT KIND OF MAN WOULD YOUR PATRON BE?

The fabulous patron. An unsentimental man, honestly acquisitive,
worked his way up from the bottom, amputated his imagination,
devoted himself to making money, assessed everything as a possible
gainer, married in order to conclude a financial deal, bought
works of art as investments, funded symphonies for tax purposes,
sired two boys because he knew he'd need a business manager and
an investment broker he could trust, pensioned off his wife when
she began to drink too much, has never been disappointed in the
boys' selfish behaviour, hopes they will thrive just as he did.
Without the encumbrance of an ethical code.

OUR READERS WOULD LOVE TO HEAR ABOUT YOUR FAVOURITE CLOTHES.

There are days when he shrinks from the squalor, the stink of dog's
urine. At any moment he can expect the landlord's voice at the

basement door, the demand for his unpaid rent. He must bestir himself. His preparations are epic:

undergarments Today he favours a rather informal style, long woollen underpants to combat the intemperate weather, his undervest a subtly matched off-white.

pants No difficulties here; he opts for the modishly torn dungarees rather than for his galligaskins, plus-fours, or toreador pants for more festive occasions.

shirt He hesitates a trifle over the pourpoint and the *gipon*, decides on a simple evening shirt, the left sleeve cunningly removed.

sweater Eschewing the cashmere and the cardigan, he chooses a crew-neck with well-ventilated bodice that allows tantalizing glimpses of the shirt and flesh beneath.

jacket Carefully he selects the delightfully *passé* Mao-jacket, rejecting the redingote, the swallowtail, and the unsuitably heavy Norfolk jacket.

overcoat Always a problem; this time, definitely, it must be the elegant raglan (discreetly lined with chic items of news reportage), not the pretentious Inverness cape, the burberry, or the serape.

hat Renowned for his headgear, he intuitively selects the French-Canadian-style *tocque* as vastly more practical than the *chateau bras*, the astrakhan, or the fedora.

socks and gloves The true sophisticate, he knows these must complement the entire ensemble; he ponders, sweating lightly, eventually decides upon thick woollen socks, gracefully ventilated at the extremities; so taken is he by this choice that he will wear a similar pair on his hands in lieu of gloves, no matter how tempting the suedes and the *mousquetaires*.

neckwear He will forego, on this occasion, the rebato, the ascot, the fichu, and plump for the tried-and-tested, charmingly unravelled, Montreal Expos comforter.

shoes Perspiration always affects this choice; what? brogans, chukka boots, perhaps? what about the hessians? the espadrilles today? the legendary *veldschoens*? the stogies? he decides ultimately upon a seasoned pair of air-freshened tennis-shoes, shrewdly perforated at the sides, insulated with well-chosen gobbets of newsprint.

Thus, dressed. Thus dressed, he sets out, with canine accompaniment, to face the world, beard the bureaucracy in its den, collect his old-age pension.

OUR READERS WOULD LOVE TO HEAR HOW THE ÉLITE SPEND A NIGHT OUT.

You fill your glass for the trillionth time, is it? marvel at the amber fluidity. You have just arrived outside the patron's mansion in the black limousine. You alone are the guest of honour at this great gathering, a fitting climax to your career. *(If only she could have been here.)* You can hear, through the car window, the twenty-piece chamber orchestra playing a mathematical selection of Bach. They are all awaiting your entrance. The chauffeur opens the door for you and you climb out, stiff at first. You are, after all, not young any more. A servant springs down from the front door to take your arm, lead you in. Through the open doorway, a drum-roll, the hubbub of excitement, the faces peering towards you. The patron appears, smiling possessively:

"My dear chap," he murmurs.

You finger your evening coat, your black tie. You prepare to be exhibited. You take the podium, accept the applause, shuffle your papers, continue:

"I have long, ladies and gentlemen, admired Sir Walter Scott…"

OUR READERS WOULD LOVE TO HEAR HOW THE ÉLITE SPEND A NIGHT AT HOME.

Now he is suddenly hungry. The excitement, perhaps. The anticipation. He ignores the attentive listeners, laden banquet tables, bowls of caviare, trays glittering with champagne. He pokes about amongst the debris that litters the apartment floor beside his chair, disturbs the dog, fishes out a package of assorted biscuits. He picks out one for himself, throws a broken piece to the anxious dog, concentrates again upon the work at hand.

THANK YOU FOR THIS. AND THANK YOU.

A Long Day in the Town

A Long Day in the Town

From this far, the buildings were nothing to me but a heap of rubble shored against the base of the mountain. It was morning in the sun. Everywhere, white scraps of butterflies trembled a foot above the ground. I kept walking, and after a while I could make out a church steeple sticking up like a dagger from the prostrate town. I walked on, as I say, uphill, always uphill, into that town, looking for the hotel. I was almost there, in the midday heat, only an occasional wisp of cloud in the bald sky. I was feeling very weary from carrying the burden of my thirst.

Then I saw a woman on the road ahead trundling a cart along behind her. She was moving so slowly that soon I was close enough to see that on her cart a corpse lay sprawled on its back, unclothed, a great creamy slug under the empty blue.

The woman stopped and waited for me. Her daughter, she sobbed, it was her twelve-year-old daughter on the cart. The woman's long brown hair was roped with sweat as though she had just given birth. She was wearing a floral dress of wilted roses. She was a thin woman, her body dangling around her. All over the corpse of the dead girl, I could see large pustules, pitched battles of flies. A white headscarf clamped the child's jaw shut, a wooden cross jutted from her stiff fingers.

I recognized the plague, the worst of deaths. I said to the woman, "Plague."

But she shouted out, "No, no!" She sobbed that her daughter was always a good girl, always full of love, and she would never leave her. She wrenched the handles of the cart away and dragged it over the cobble-stones up towards the town.

I walked behind her, watching how, after every few dozen steps, she would lay down the handles and take a damp yellow rag from her pocket. She would shoo away the flies and tenderly begin to wipe the face of her daughter, cooing and smiling to her, alert for any sign of life.

As we entered the town, some of the townswomen, black headscarves over stocky bodies, came out to their doors to see her passing by. With soft voices, they crooned, "Ah well, she's dead now and you must bury her." They told her she would never wipe death away with a wet cloth.

But she kept shouting, "No, no!" She told them, sobbing, that she was a raped woman, raped from inside by sorrow. She said she was a woman dying of hunger, starving to death, for her daughter was her only food. But always they repeated to her, "Ah well, she's dead now and you must bury her."

By this point, we were near the town hotel, so I left these women to their sad dialogue whilst I booked a room. When I came out a few minutes later, the street was empty. There was a little park opposite, so I brought a mug of beer and sat on the park bench. A few gangling trees grew in that park, and grass brown with drought.

For an hour, nothing happened (I, on the bench, sipped my beer, transforming myself gradually into a human oasis; above, the sun journeyed on its way a thousand more miles; at my feet, a regiment of black ants on the dusty path dismembered a solitary caterpillar), then a bearded man of about twenty-five sat down beside me, his head motionless, his eyes scanning back and forth like a searchlight, resting on me for a moment at the end of each lateral swing. He wore a black dress suit, stained down the front, rotted with sweat at the armpits.

"You're not one of them," he said in a whisper, hardly moving his lips.

I showed no interest.

"No, you couldn't be, not this soon," and I could see that he had convinced himself of something, and felt secure.

Then he began to talk, determined to tell me what was on his mind.

He said he had good reason to trust no one. He and his two brothers and a sister had been raised on a poor scrub-farm. He was the youngest child, unwanted by his mother and despised by his father, who, he said, looked very like him. It still disgusted him, he said, this likeness. He could not help feeling his father in himself — his hands, his face, his nervous ticks.

When he turned twelve years old, the others made up their minds, as a family, to murder him (he had seen it coming). Yes, he assured me, they began their efforts to kill him at the age of twelve.

Their first attempt was clumsy but unambiguous. One morning, his brothers, who had spoken to him only to insult him for as long as he could remember, began to encourage him to eat up his porridge. At the same time, they tried not to show too much interest, not to look at his plate. His parents and his sister loosed a smoke-screen of chit-chat through which, nonetheless, he could make out the glitter in their eyes.

He decided not to eat the porridge. Instead, he put the plate on the floor for the black-and-white farm collie. They all stopped talking and watched intently, his father, his mother, his brothers, his sister, as the dog, after eating, began to whimper and convulse, and in a few minutes fell on its side, dead.

No one made any comment.

After that first failed attempt to poison him, the family made an honest effort in those early days to arrange his murder in ways that might be mistaken, by others at least, for accidents. He remembered his brothers trying to force his head below water in the swimming hole. He managed to slither and squirm free for his life. His remembered his sister thrusting him one morning through the hayloft door as they were lowering bales to the trailer far below. He grabbed the chains of the pulley, swinging for a moment, like a hanged man, before shinning up to safety. He remembered other attempts: the pushes into the flailing arms of the thresher; into the knacker's bubbling cauldron; into the paddock of a rampant bull. Each time he escaped.

Yet he continued to live with them, intimate with his murderers, a scared boy, not knowing what else to do. He became used to their attempts on his life. He became skilled, like an animal, in avoiding his predators, taking their menace for granted, learning how to defend himself, always alert. He never knowingly let them get behind him. He relied on his hearing, smell, taste. He became quick and tough, so that after each murderous attempt, he was harder than ever to kill. Asleep, he was a watch-dog, pricked awake by the creak of a tree, the wind's rustle.

When he turned fourteen, they changed their tactics.

One day as he was working in the high-walled vegetable garden behind the house with his brothers and sister, he noticed, too late, his father and mother at the kitchen window, looking out with great interest.

Before he could move, one of his brothers leapt on him and wrestled him down onto the potato drills, kneeling on his arms. His sister ran over and straddled herself across his legs. Then the eldest brother, seventeen years old, who had never called him by his first name in all his life, put his thick hands around his neck and began to choke the breath out of him.

He did the only thing he could, he made a desperate kicking motion, landing his knee right in the fork of his sister's spindly legs (she was her mother's daughter), so that she screamed out in pain and crashed into the younger brother. He was able to wriggle out of their grasp and run to the corner of the garden, at bay, with a pitchfork in his hands. They all looked towards the window where his parents watched. His father stared for a while, then shook his head slowly. The elder brother reluctantly opened the garden gate and went away, followed by his brother and sister, she limping and sobbing, to go about their day's work. Nothing was said.

But he knew now he could not stay. That night he packed a potato sack with his few clothes, crept out into the darkness, and left his home forever.

That was only the beginning, twelve years ago. Since then, they had tracked him down, time after time, no matter where he went, determined to finish him off. By now, they had tried innumerable ways to kill him. As he had become an expert survivor, they had become skilled assassins. In a steamy Malaysian swamp, for instance, they had grazed his back with their parangs. In Patagonia, they had almost entangled his nimble feet with a set of leather bolas. In a midnight alleyway in Istanbul, they had dangerously wounded him in the shoulder with yataghans. In Madrid, twice in a single day, they had inflicted severe injuries on his naked flesh with a misericord and a bilbo. In the Scottish Highlands, they almost had him, partially pinning his coat sleeve to a wall with expertly thrown skean dhus. Once, in the veldt of southern Africa, they had barely missed him with a hail of deadly assegais. He, in turn, had beaten off their shillelagh-attack in Phoenix Park, Dublin.

In every corner of the globe they had ambushed him with Gatling guns or Thompson sub-machine-guns. In one hemisphere they had almost slipped a garotte around his scrawny neck. In another, they missed him, but eliminated five hundred innocents by means of a limpet-mine on a trans-ocean crossing. One night, in Borneo, he detected, just in time, a cunningly placed castrator mine they had hidden in the toilet bowl of his hotel room.

As for poisons, they had tried wolfsbane in his beer, banewort in his Ovaltine, aconite in his ham and eggs, bearded darnel in his bread pudding, corn cackle in his angel cake, death angel in his cornflakes. Still he had survived.

As he told me all this, he never stopped looking around the park, his right ear cocked for any sound, like a morning bird on a summer lawn.

"You're sure you're not one of them?" he asked again, flicking at me with his eyes.

He told me how he had once fallen in love with a prostitute. Night after night they had made love, becoming a marvellous machine. But one night, in the middle of the night, he woke by some instinct to see her reared above him with a pair of scissors in her hand, tears streaming down her face, about to stab him. He jumped clear, realizing with horror that the prostitute was his own sister. He himself had been a master at spotting her disguises, never so nearly failing until now.

So he had come here, to play for time, to decide on his next move. He had heard of this town by chance, he had heard that a life here was no life, and they might leave him alone at last. Yet he often wondered what he would do with himself, what he would do with his life, if they left him alone.

I waited till he was finished, then asked him if he had any idea why they had spent all those years trying to kill him. He looked at me, puzzled. Even, perhaps, with pity. I could see he thought I must be a madman, and that my question made no sense to him, no sense at all.

He rose to go, saying he'd been exposed here in the park long enough, looking me up and down, his bird-head twitching. Then he left, picking his way through the park as though it was a minefield.

The air was suddenly chilly. I looked up, and saw that the mountain had already lopped off part of the early afternoon sun. So I crossed the street again to the hotel, a dilapidated three-storey building. The outside was brick except for a few feet of stone at the bottom, like a pair of socks. A single turret above the entrance was a finger, stained from scooping decades of dust out of the air.

Inside, the furniture, distorted pieces of plastic passing for chairs and tables, was worn as though from overuse. Yet I was the only guest, and the room-clerk assured me the town had never been busy. Disembodied smells wandered the corridors, needing exorcism by fresh air.

In the evening I went down to the dark cellar that was the hotel bar, and tried, unsuccessfully, to chat with the bartender, a man whose hands quivered constantly and who spoke so rapidly he seemed to say everything in machine-gun bursts of sound. His tone of voice was friendly, though his face was nothing but a scar adorned with eyes and mouth. He served my drink, spilling much of it over the table.

Around eight o'clock, a woman of great beauty wearing an elegant summer dress came in and ordered a drink. She looked towards me, and came and sat beside me.

We talked for some time, a camouflage of noise, neither of us revealing our positions. Only one thing she made plain: she liked to spend time with strangers in the bar, and she liked nothing better than to spend the night with them in their beds.

When she had drunk enough, we left the bar and its tremulous keeper and groped our way through the smells up the dim flight of stairs. We plodded along the spongy corridor to the dark room allotted to me out of all the other rooms in that hotel.

I closed the door. She stood in the middle of the floor and began to undress without hurry, allowing her fashionable summer dress and her bra to fall carelessly on top of her sandals. She smiled at me, her body beautifully symmetrical, her skin brown, her breasts slightly drooping, mature and brown, her legs shapely, a space between them at her crotch. She wriggled out of her pants, exposing the pubic hair, shaved neatly to accommodate the slight swimsuit whose outline I could see bracketing her groin.

She took my hand and walked me towards the bed. She lay down and watched whilst I removed my own clothing, carefully folding each item and placing it on a chair in the exact order in which I would later put it back on. Then I lay down on the side of the bed nearest the black, fetal telephone.

I took her in my arms. That was when I noticed the first faint scar, as I was kissing her neck, the smell of her perfume in my nostrils. A very fine scar it was, running along the side of her jawbone all the way from her ear to the tip of her chin, and on past the tip, up to the other ear. There it connected with a faint scar running all along the scalp line of her hair. I looked at her face, and saw now, on the bridge of her nose, the very fine scars in the shape of a cross, an insignia.

She seemed unaware, so far, of my inspection and was becoming more active, fondling me. So I moved down her body, noticing now, like a fisherman glimpsing trout in dark waters, the fine group of scars around the bases of her breasts and the smaller scars ringing the nipples that were now erect under my fingers. I traced, as I progressed down her body, the long fine scar that ran from the breast-bone, traversing a cross-hatching of delicate horizontal scars patterned on her stomach, deep into the pubic hair.

Between her legs, I saw two long dainty scars sweeping from the vulva along the inside of her thighs to her knees.

I turned her gently onto her stomach. With heightened acuity, I immediately noted the scars that curved around her buttocks, shapely scimitars sweeping from the hips in towards the cleft of the anus. I saw too the long elegant scars that ran from her waist towards the shaven, perfumed armpits.

She had stopped her writhing, and was enduring my inspection. She turned over. I looked into her eyes, searching for her. Behind the fashionable mascara I could see the ancient sadness of those eyes. She sighed, and her left arm swept her long black hair onto the pillow behind two ears of almost identical shapes. Her right arm lay across her breasts as she spoke, selecting each word as though it were a scalpel:

"I am a patchwork woman. I was so ugly I had to put a wall round myself to keep others from seeing me. I was made beautiful by surgery. But the scars are judases. I used to think my heart would die, but it always lets me down.

"I came to this town in the end thinking that someone who chose to live in this place might be willing to love me. But they use me here like a rubber doll, a good invention, life-size, but not a woman."

After she had spoken, I rose from her, and began to dress myself carefully, smoothing each garment into place, checking myself constantly in the rusted mirror, gauging with my fingertips the soft texture of my cheeks, patting the stray hairs into place. I went out into the silence of the drab corridor, without looking back, and closed the door firmly.

When I returned a few hours later, the room was empty and I did not go looking for the woman.

The next morning was bright and sunny. A stale roll and a cup of tepid coffee in the hotel restaurant convinced me I was not hungry. I went outside, wading ankle-deep in butterflies to the park bench where I sat down in the soothing morning heat.

A man of middle height, not old, black curls, came and sat beside me on the bench. Lunar craters pitted his face.

When he saw that I was staring at him, he leaned over, his whole body rustling, and asked in a foreign accent if I would give him money for coffee. I could see that the rustling came from scraps of paper stuffed under his clothes, protruding at the neck and the placket of his shirt, stuccoing his sleeves and trouser-legs.

He apologized for "the inconvenient noise" of these papers under his clothes, saying he was a poet. When he was working on a poem, he said, he would write down on separate scraps of paper each of the words he intended to use, and tape them to various parts of his body. It was bad luck to reveal which parts of the body were more effective for certain words, and anyway, he was still at the exploration stage. He hoped I would forgive his reticence.

He only knew that, in a few days, he would feel the words were permeated by him, he by the words. They would possess each other intimately, he would *become* a poem with human organs.

I took him back to the hotel restaurant which had been given over now, in the morning heat, to a convention of bluebottles. He fought with them for the remnants of hardening bread, and drank down cup after cup of lukewarm coffee, holding the cup in both hands, till beads of sweat acknowledged the labour of eating and drinking.

He began to talk about his past. How, at university, he had come to idolize an outspoken group of writers and thinkers. How one of them, a poet, had told him, "A real poet is a terrorist, a knee-capper, a mixer of Molotov-cocktails, a man who NEVER writes a poem." How, in the excitement of it all, he had become a member of a cell of anarchists. How, in a basement room, he had chosen the straw that singled him out to blow up the police headquarters surrounded by high electrified fences, and battlements of sandbags. How, next day, he had walked softly up to the entrance of the headquarters with his hands above his head. How the guards had searched him thoroughly, he beseeching them not to handle him roughly. How he dared not flinch when they had probed his anus for a weapon. How they could not have guessed that he himself *was* the weapon.

He had been transformed into the weapon ten minutes before he had presented himself at the headquarters. In a nearby apartment, his friends had poured, with the utmost care, through a long plastic tube down his throat and into his stomach, a litre of nitroglycerine. All that he had to do was to walk into the headquarters and bruise himself against any object, or tumble to the floor, or jump up and down, and a fifty-yards-wide chasm would be created around him.

But, there in the headquarters, he changed his mind. Everything changed when he suddenly realized, right there inside the target, that all he had ever wanted to be was a poet, all the time, an old-fashioned poet, a writer of poems. It was like meeting himself for the first time, saying "How do you do?" to himself at long last.

Yet there he was, the major actor in a nightmare-drama in which he no longer wished to say his lines. To tremble would mean obliteration. He was almost afraid to speak in case his epiglottis detonated him. So he signalled, ever so cautiously, to one of the policemen, and whispered the plot. The policeman saw his terror and knew he told the truth.

Within minutes (during which a huge hairy insect, nausea, began to creep over his stomach and intestines, during which he glimpsed, sadly, the beauty of a dozen fleeing faces, the last he would ever see, during which he felt the warmth of the sunbeams streaming through the windows above him, alive with atoms of light), the headquarters were empty.

Then he couldn't hold it in anymore. He vomited up the nitro-glycerine, it erupted from him, spouted into the air, and curved to the floor in front of him with a great sloshing splash.

And nothing happened. No void, no annihilation, no negation of being. Only a sick boy, shuddering with nausea, wishing he were dead. Something had gone wrong, he realized. His terrorist friends should have remained poets: the nitro they had filled him with was contaminated, useless. He might just as well have chugged down a litre of camel-piss for all the chance it had of exploding.

So he betrayed them all. When, after many hours, the police cautiously returned to the building, he was determined to talk. He told every name, every last one of them, and when he saw the disappointment of the police at how little he knew, he told more, making up incidents, incriminating friends and enemies alike, anyone who could testify to his foolishness, anyone unfortunate enough to have been in his past, wiping his life behind him clean, like a slate, so that he would have no past to haunt him. And all the while loving it, loving the lying, loving the obligation to lie, feeling like a poet once again.

Now, in the restaurant, he began eating once more, a hungry poet, fatigued by his memories. As I left, he was squabbling with the bluebottles over the relics of breakfast.

That night, around midnight, I saw something that frightened me, and I decided to leave that town as soon as possible.

I had gone out for some fresh air, but a thick fog obscured even the little park across from the hotel. Further up the street, the haze of the street lamps shone faintly, and I walked towards them.

Soon, I could hear shuffling sounds, and I could make out something huge swaying down the street under the lurid lights. Noises came from all along its length, a monster of many mouths talking to itself.

From the shelter of a house door, I was relieved to see that it was only a mass of the townspeople slowly shambling along the street. Many of them were contorted into grotesque postures, supported by crutches, and canes, and all the iron paraphernalia of pain. The laboured breathing in the heavy fog was a chilling chorus. They advanced cautiously, as though the street was a quicksand, and they had to be careful to step only on the solid parts.

All at once, all of the faces turned to look in my direction. I could not be certain in that light, but I thought I recognized some of them: the hotel bartender, the mother of the plague victim, the man whose family sought his death, the woman with the scars, the traitor-poet, all of them looking towards me. The moaning became more highly pitched, the whole procession swayed towards where I stood. Many stretched their arms out towards me, but without menace, their eyes, their mouths, smiling, as though to welcome a friend.

I turned away and began to walk, as quickly as I could, back to the hotel, where I locked myself in my room, propping a chair against the door handle. All night I could hear the creaking of footsteps on the carpeted corridor, soft tapping on my door and even my window. I could hear unpleasant laughter. I heard it all, for I did not sleep.

Next morning, I left the town behind me for good. The sun was up early, an orange eye with cataracts in the eastern sky. From several miles away across the plain, I looked back, a last look at the town, a pile of rubble from here, heaped against the base of the mountain with its misty top. I made a clenched fist of my brain and kept walking, walking, up to my knees at times in a vast, shallow lagoon of butterflies, till I could see ahead of me the green plain that stretched, far away, to another horizon.

Twins

Twins

People swarm from north and south, abandon the rituals of Saturday afternoon shopping expeditions and ball-game attendances, in favour of him. One thing: no children. He demands no admission fee, so he is entitled to say "No children." ("Say" won't do. Even that woman, his mother, the crutch on which he has limped his eighteen years, can never be sure of what he "says." He, therefore, writes. And has written, with his right hand, and with his left hand, "NO CHILDREN.") For children are always the enemy: they suspect something, frown at him, tire of his performances, spoil everything. (As for dogs, they are wary too when they see him out walking. They sheath their tails. They slink growling to the opposite side of the road.) But, ah! The adults! The benches of the old church hall sag under the weight of their veneration. His devotees. How they admire him, how they nod their approval of his enigmatic sermons. He bestows upon them tears perhaps of gratitude, howls perhaps of execration. Either way, his votaries (the tall man with the blue eyes sits among them) are content.

The name of the one they come to hear? Malachi. That, at least, is sure. He has a sickness (is there a name for it?). His sickness attracts them. He is the one who speaks with two voices, two different voices, at the same time. One of the voices trolls smoothly from the right side of his mouth. The other crackles from the left corner. How memorable, how remarkable, the sound of those two voices emanating from that one flexible mouth.

Is his affliction, then, a miracle? No matter, it certainly complicates his life. It might be easier to bear if the two voices would speak in turns. But whenever he wants to say something, both voices chime in, overlap, each using an exactly equal number of syllables. Without euphony. There is discord in the sounds, there is dissent in the things said. What allures is the eeriness of it. The right-side voice thanks the tall man with the blue eyes for a gift he has brought:

"Thanks a lot."

But the left-side voice remarks simultaneously:

"You're a fool."

(Or is it vice-versa? Often it is hard to tell.) The hearing is a difficult experience. Words sometimes twine together, like this —

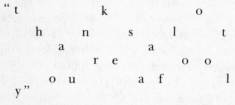

— braided like two snakes. Or a discrepancy in timing produces a long, alien word: "*thyaounksreaalfoolot.*" Or exact synchronization causes a triple grunt: "*th$_y$a$_{ou}$nks$_{re}$a$_a$lf$_o$°t$_{ol}$.*" Leaving the hearer to rummage among fragments of words, palimpsests of phrases. Did he hear, "you're a lot," "thanks a fool," "yanks a lol," "thou're a foot?"

A disease of words. When Malachi was a child, nobody was willing to diagnose his problem. No father to turn to. His mother never revealed who fathered him in the bed of her clapboard house, imitation brick, a mile north of town. Malachi squirmed out of the womb, purple. Let loose his inhuman shrieks. It was presumed his brain was not right.

See him at the age of ten. A boy unable to cope with anything scholastic. No one understands his noises, the drooling, the maddening grunts. Then, lying on the floor on a Sunday morning in June, in his mother's presence, tiger stripes of sun through the shutters on his prone body, he who has never written a word, picks up two pencils, one in each hand, and writes two messages simultaneously on a sheet of paper. With his right hand, a neat firm line:

"Help me, Mother."

With his left hand a scrawl:

"Leave me alone."

She stares at the paper, squints at his mouth, understands at last.

The why of it? How can such a thing have happened to her son? She expounds her theory to the tall man. (He has blue eyes, fine lines web the corners.) Malachi, she says, is meant to be twins, but somehow the division has not occurred, and he has been born, two people condemned to one body. Reverse Siamese twins. When she speaks of her theory in Malachi's presence, his face seems to confirm it. The right side blooms smooth, an innocent boy's. The left side shimmers with defiance. His head becomes unsteady, wobbles like an erratic planet with orbiting satellite eyes.

The German pastor is the force behind the audiences. He has spoken at some length to the tall man with the unflinching blue eyes. The pastor suggests to the mother that it will be good for the boy's confidence to exhibit himself. Is the pastor concerned about therapy or theology? Is he convinced that ultimately one voice or the other will prevail in open combat? Is he enthusiastic because he himself marvels at the sight? (Understands something?) He never misses an audience, sits rapt, engrossed in the turmoil in the face, the voice, of Malachi.

A sudden change. In the middle of the eighteenth year, tranquillity. The harsh voice silent, the soft voice alone emerges from the twisted mouth, unencumbered. The left side of the mouth still curls, the left cheek still twitches, the left eye still glares. People still cringe ready for the snarl. But they wait in vain. And Malachi appears one morning wearing a black cloth patch over the left side of his face. A black triangle.

They ask him, "What has happened to your other voice?"

He seems surprised at the question, as though unaware of the years of struggle. Soon, no one asks him any more, everyone becomes used to his masked face. They admire it, a portentous half moon. Malachi is a kind-hearted boy. His long illness is forgotten.

Three years later, he dies. At the age of twenty-one, he is sucked into the spirals of the river on a dark night. The verdict at the inquest: death by accident. The pathologist does not fail to take note of Malachi's remarkable tongue, wide as two normal tongues, linked by a membrane of skin. It must have made breathing difficult in those final moments. Malachi's mother attends the inquest, too distraught to be called as a witness. Afterwards, in the car park, the tall man catches up to her. He is about her age. (He has blue eyes. Fine lines web the corners.) He is silent. The sun beats down, mid-July, a day that ridicules mourning. She is still a woman of some beauty.

"It would have happened long ago," she says, "but for a pact. Three years ago I made them agree to it. One voice was to be in command all day, then after dark the other would take over. They just shifted the patch. But the girl drove them against each other again. They were jealous over her. They couldn't share her any longer. They needed to fight it out. But there was only the one body to hurt."

She can no longer control herself. She sobs, and begs the man to leave her alone. A neighbour takes her by the arm to a waiting car. The man with blue eyes watches her go. He knows what must be done.

He drives to where the girl lives, a country motel, a run-down place, peeling green paint. She greets him solemnly, invites him up to her room. A lank-haired girl, not beautiful. He savours her quiet voice.

"He was a good friend to me," telling of Malachi. "I could trust him. On sunny days, we just sat by the river and talked. He said everything was under control. I was not to worry about his moods at night. I told him I liked him just as much at night when he switched the patch and changed his voice. At night, he would drink and drink, and make love. I told him how much I loved the feel of his tongue on my body. I suppose he didn't believe me."

She asks the man with the blue eyes to wait with her for a while. He stays, consoles her. It is dark when he leaves.

Ten years have passed. I am on an assignment to this country town. It is a pleasant summer's morning with, strangely, an arc of moon still visible in the bright sky like a single heelprint on glare ice. I am here to observe two children. They are twins, I am told. I am a little afraid of what I may find. I have a fear of children.

They don't look especially alike. One is fair, composed, the other dark and fidgety. They are ten years old. They speak in a babble no one has been able to understand. Aside from themselves, that is, for they seem to understand each other.

I am here with the other observers because of a curious development. The twins have discovered how to communicate with the world. When they wish to be understood by others, we are told, they join hands and speak in unison. The sounds blend together and produce words that are intelligible.

The twins do not seem happy to meet our group of linguists, philologists, semanticists, etymologists, cynics, believers. Amongst us, the tall man with blue eyes. Fine lines web the corners. He seems anxious.

At length the boys' mother, who has not changed much over the years, asks them to speak to us. They hesitate, resolve to please her. They join hands. The two solo voices that, separately, are incomprehensible to the audience, blend together in a curious duet:

"Please help us, Father," they cry.

This evokes great delight on the part of the other observers. They demand more. But the two little boys stand firm, hand-in-hand. They look directly at me. They repeat, for me, their shy, angry chant:

"Please help us, Father," they plead.

They are staring directly at the man with blue eyes. He glances around fearfully, understands that the boys are making their appeal only to him. He looks at me in desperation. He can no longer refuse to acknowledge me. I, for my part, am ready to acknowledge him. I try to control my terror. I extend my hand to him. I find I am alone. Alone, for the first time, with my children.

The Fugue

The Fugue

Where are the beginnings, the endings, and most important, the middles?

Cortazar

Knowing it well, the cedar-timbered house high on the river bank. That a man would be there at this time of day. That he would be alone in the house, its backyard descending to the river in stages. His mind explored it for the thousandth time. On the top level, a lawn with a few apple trees still in blossom spread itself out from the walls of the house. Next, a thicket of uncultivated bush acted as a kind of natural barrier, penetrated by a rough path to the edge of the plateau. Finally, a wooden staircase of fifty rotted steps tottered down the steep embankment of weeds and brambles to an overgrown lane by the riverside. This was the lane on which he stood, invisible from the house, used mainly by dog-walkers and fishermen. Lovers too. Lovers. Anger began to seep through, he must breathe deeply, be calm. His fingers circled the hand-rail, and he began to climb the stairs with exaggerated caution, though no sound he made would reach the house. At the top he paused. Now, as ever, there was no turning back. He advanced with care through the belt of bush till he could see the well-trimmed lawn powdered with apple blossoms, and, dominating everything, the cedar walls of the house. The chill of the steel knife-blade tucked into his trouser-waist comforted him, slowed the pounding of his heart. He slid from the cover of one tree to the next until he was able to peer into the downstairs study with its long picture-window and adjacent sliding-door. Elation. There he sat, in the study, as expected, his head showing above the stuffed armchair, its back towards the window. Stealthily he worked his way closer to the house, making use of the intervening trees. The last few yards, he lunged forward, pressing his body against the section of wall between the window and the door. He tensed himself, held his breath. No noise from inside. He had not been seen. A quick squint showed the man still secure in his chair, the back of his greying head magnified from this close. Reading. On a heavy wooden side-table at his right hand stood a tumbler of what must be Scotch — he liked his Scotch — still nearly full. He was a man of habit, would read for an hour then take his nap. Another squint to check that all was well. From this far he could not make out the book, doubtless some cheap novel, the kind he loved, though he masqueraded as a scholar and a man of culture. Deceiving those who could know no better. Bitterness must not prevent him, especially now, from thinking clearly. Gently he tested the sliding door. It slid noiselessly on its well-oiled tracks, as he knew it would. On such a windless day, no draught would betray his intrusion. The man was preoccupied with his reading, quite unaware that someone was now in the room behind him, gliding silently towards his chair, holding a knife warm from the heat of his body, eyes glinting. All his attention was concentrated on the book before him.

Marvelling, for the thousandth time, at the delight reading gave him. To lose himself in a book, savouring the characters, the plot, the words. He often felt that for him fiction was a necessary escape from the unpleasant reality of his own personality. For though he admired the romantic qualities of fictional heroes such as the well-meaning detective in this book, he had no urge to emulate them. He preferred in his own life to get what he wanted by any means he could. He enjoyed these wishful fantasies of an ordered universe, but understood the world well enough to know their place in his own particular jungle. He wondered, with amusement, whether it was possible for a man to squander, quite vicariously in reading, all his human potential, and then to return to reality as he himself always did, calloused and even more cynical. It was ironic that people enthused over the great empathy and sensitivity he showed in his critical writings. They had certainly ensured his success in academic circles, most of all with women. Those cultured, naïve women fell for him, often aspiring female graduate students or the wives of colleagues. They presumed that despite his hard shell a man of such understanding could never abuse their love. She had begged him to invite her here not two weeks ago — to discuss her term paper. Well. They both knew what that meant. No sooner had she had a drink than she was writhing in his arms coaxing him up to the bedroom. All the time adoring him with her eyes as though she had found the Holy Grail and not the same man who'd already had it off with her best friend last semester. Surely she knew he desired nothing more than a bit of variety. And variety she supplied, with her ardour and her agility. But a nuisance. Insisting he treat her as more than the obligatory spring-season lay. He'd sent her packing back to her boyfriend a little sooner than he'd meant to. He was not tolerant of such an inability to separate natural cravings from romantic delusions. Now take the hero of this novel: he was an idealist, but that was exactly as it should be in fiction. This policeman was committed to some principle of justice, no matter how vaguely understood, and his sense of duty forced him to offer the protection of the law to everyone, even to those he despised. Here he was now in the predictable climactic confrontation scene of the novel, agonizing over his role, yet heroically carrying on.

Urging the squad-car driver to get there as quickly as possible. Though they were not far away, the heavy traffic frustrated their efforts. Yet he had to forbid the use of the siren for fear of precipitating the crime. He could only hope they would not be too late, otherwise he might have on his conscience a man's life, a man not altogether guiltless. For the thousandth time he put this thought out of his mind. It was not his responsibility to judge final guilt or innocence, so why make a hard job unbearable? At last the car swung off the main road onto one of the quiet suburban streets near the river, then into the familiar heavily treed crescent, the lawns glistening with sprinklers, fruit trees remarkable in their spring bloom. He was thankful he could still savour such things, no matter what unpleasantness lay ahead. The car drew up in front of the house. It struck him how easy it would be for someone to approach from the rear unseen, and he leapt from the car and ran quickly round to the backyard. No one. He strode across the lawn, looking down the path towards the river. No sign of an intruder. Perhaps her fears were groundless, the delusions of a wronged woman. He turned towards the house and at once the open sliding-door assaulted his eyes. Now, through the picture-window, he saw everything. One of them sat in an armchair, his head slightly bowed, all his attention riveted on a book. Behind him stood the other, a knife raised ready to strike. Time suspended them all. Then the knife began its smooth arc. He hesitated for a particle of a second, raised the revolver and squeezed the trigger.

PENGUIN · SHORT · FICTION

Other Titles In This Series

Other Titles In This Series

PENGUIN · SHORT · FICTION

Other Titles In This Series